Wakefield Press

Many Years a Thief

David Hutchison was born in Perth, Western Australia, in 1927, and now lives in Fremantle. He is married and has a daughter and a son. David has degrees in civil engineering and history, and a Diploma of Education, and has taught physics, lectured on the history and philosophy of science, and was an adult educator. In 1970 he became the first Curator of History at the Western Australian Museum, and is an Inaugural Honorary Fellow of the National Museum of Australia.

David Hutchison retired in 1985 to work as a museologist and heritage consultant. His publications include articles, essays, poetry, short fiction, botanical illustrations, *A Town Like No Other* (about the Benedictine Community of New Norcia in Western Australia), and *Fremantle Walks*.

Also by this author

A Town Like No Other: The Living Traditions of New Norcia,
1995 (editor)

Fremantle Walks, 2006

Many Years
a Thief

David Hutchison

**Wakefield
Press**

Wakefield Press
1 The Parade West
Kent Town
South Australia 5067
www.wakefieldpress.com.au

First published 2007
Copyright © David Hutchison 2007

Cover designed by Liz Nicholson, designBITE
Designed and typeset by Clinton Ellicott, Wakefield Press
Printed in Australia by Griffin Press, Adelaide

National Library of Australia
Cataloguing-in-publication entry

Hutchison, David.
Many years a thief.

ISBN 978 1 86254 746 9 (pbk.).

I. Title.

A823.4

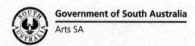
Government of South Australia
Arts SA

Publication of this book was assisted by the
Commonwealth Government through the
Australia Council, its arts funding and advisory body.

*Dedicated to my wife June
and my children Jane and Mark,
with gratitude for love and support.*

Preface

The Colony of Western Australia did not receive transported adult convicts until 1850, but 234 juvenile convicts from the Parkhurst Reformatory, on the Isle of Wight, were transported there from 1842 to 1851. Because most of the early settlers did not want to live in a convict colony, the boys were called 'Government Juvenile Immigrants'.

John Schoales, an Anglo–Irish lawyer, was appointed the guardian of these boys when the first batch arrived on the *Simon Taylor* in 1842. At that time, he was just thirty-two years old. His words to Governor Hutt, written on 1 January 1845, express the burden of his charge:

Too much must not be demanded or expected. It is not in the power of men to work the thorough reformation of his fellow Mortal. It is the Almighty alone who can touch and subdue the heart. Man may compel the suppression of open displays of Sin and Vice, even though the disposition to offend remains. But there his power stops. He may teach, may indicate, but he cannot command.

Ash Wednesday, 1865

Although Pinjarra now had a church, there was no hall where parishioners could gather socially, so Mrs Holland invited the ladies to her house to mark Ash Wednesday. When they had all arrived, she read, in lieu of grace, the Ash Wednesday collect.

'Almighty and everlasting God, who hatest nothing that thou hast made, and dost forgive the sins of all them that are penitent; create and make in us new and contrite hearts, that we, worthily lamenting our sins, and acknowledging our wretchedness, may obtain of thee, the God of all mercy, perfect remission and forgiveness; through Jesus Christ our Lord.'

Some of the women said 'Amen' loudly and clearly; others mumbled and glanced at the table on which were a large enamel teapot, a milk jug, thick white china cups and a large plate of scones – plain with a scrape of jam but no cream, because it was Lent. In the marri trees outside Mrs Holland's house, the black cockatoos squabbled as they ransacked the green gumnuts.

'They're devilish birds,' Mrs O'Neil said. 'Black, and the red in their tails, like fire.'

Mrs Lewis glanced out the window. 'They were there then. It was years ago . . . twenty-one years . . . when I saw him.'

'Who, Missus Lewis?' Mrs Holland asked. 'Who did you see?'

'The devil.'

'The devil?'

'The devil himself.' Mrs Lewis spoke in a low voice; only Mrs Holland and two other women near to her noticed the sudden change in her tone. Those two stopped talking, and the other women fell quiet with teacups or scones arrested halfway to their lips, wondering what Mrs Lewis had said to make the silence that followed her words so fraught with disquiet.

Mrs O'Neil, Irish but pugnaciously Protestant, spoke first. 'The devil you say, Missus Lewis? The devil!' It sounded like an oath. 'What did he look like, now? Was there fire and brimstone?'

'There was fire, and smoke ... so thick I couldn't see where she was ... Jane. That was before I knew that he was the devil.'

There was deep grieving in her voice now, enough to convince Mrs O'Neil that she had seen something.

'A fire, but no brimstone?'

'No brimstone. Ash, though ... like grey snow after the fire.'

'Did he stand in the flames? Did he have horns and a tail, a forked tail?'

'No! Not *in* the fire. No horns ... no tail. He looked like a boy, with a strange head ... bulging like this.' She took off her black mobcap, revealing dense, waved, white hair, and held it at the back of her head to simulate a distortion of her skull. 'I didn't know at first.'

'Didn't know what?'

'That he was the devil.'

'When did you ... how did you know?' Mrs O'Neil was determined to get to the bottom of it. She would have been offended if she had seen that one of the other women crossed herself, her pale, thin hand fluttering like a bird trying to perch on her bosom.

'I knew it afterward, knew it was him, by what he did. It was Ash Wednesday then, too. The ashes of the fire were still there.' Her mind seemed to be wandering, and she was clearly pained by the recollection.

The other women murmured in sympathy and wonder, uneasy that they had begun Lent by talking of the devil. Mrs O'Neil, however, was dogged.

'But, if he had no horns, no ...'

'It was the deaths ... two so soon ... then next year, Charlie. My first husband, John Pollard, was alive then.'

'Pollard!' Mrs Holland blurted out.

'How could you be sure?' Mrs O'Neil persisted.

'Hush now, Missus O'Neil,' Mrs Holland said, raising her hand to gesture for quiet, although, as she turned her palm toward Mrs Lewis, she may also have been blessing.

Mrs O'Neil looked uncomfortable but fell silent.

Mrs Lewis stood up suddenly, raising her hands to her bosom; they were pallid against the black of her widow's weeds, donned recently after the death of her second husband. She reached suddenly for her reticule and hymn-book, and knocked over her cup. She took a handkerchief from her sleeve and mopped up the small splash of tea.

'Don't worry about that,' Mrs Holland said. She may have

addressed the remark to Mrs O'Neil, who seemed to be about to ask another question as Mrs Lewis prepared to leave.

After she had left, the ladies turned toward Mrs Holland, who gathered herself and said, 'I remember now. It was a terrible tragedy, on a farm on the Dandalup. It must have been about twenty years ago. I didn't know that Missus Lewis had been Missus Pollard, the poor woman!'

Mrs Lewis left Mrs Holland's house and walked toward her cottage at the south end of the village, which some had begun to call a town. She muttered, 'Why did God spare me?' and wondered if it was blasphemy to question His will.

She bent to smell a rose at the fence of a neighbour's garden. She buried her small, beaked nose in the dense cluster of dark-red petals, inhaling the aroma, like strong, sweet tea. She plucked the flower and walked on, holding it to her nose.

'Why did he spare me?' she spoke aloud, and appeared to be addressing the rose.

After a few paces, she lowered it and, after contemplating it for a while, began to pluck the petals one by one, her fingers becoming stained deep red at the tips.

'Did he spare me? He didn't. He did. He didn't . . .'

She sighed, remembering those deaths: Jane, George, her baby Charlie, and her first husband, John . . . and poor John Schoales. They were all too young to die. She was saddened to think how many years had been stolen from them.

A black cat ran across her path. She crossed herself and tossed away the half-plucked rose.

I

John Schoales thrust out an arm to hold down the papers on his desk as a sudden gust of wind came through the open window. The gale had changed direction, and now blew from the north-east across the wide reach of the Swan River in front of Perth. The bluff of Mount Eliza, immediately to the west of the town, no longer sheltered the steam mill, which was on the narrow land between it and the river. The storm was unseasonable, although the seasons themselves were out of kilter in this topsy-turvy land.

When there was a lull, he went to the window and struggled to shut it, but the frame had jammed. He managed at last, excluding the wind but not its threatening roar. He kept his office in buildings near the mill, although he and his brother-in-law, Richard Nash, had sold the machinery when their joint venture had proved unprofitable. As had his trip to England as an immigration agent two years ago.

The rain was now very heavy. He was glad that the storm had not come the previous day, when he returned from several days riding to visit some of the Government Juvenile Immigrants – his wards as he now called them – who had been assigned to masters.

He turned the pages of his desk calendar to check the day's date, and then wrote it at the head of a report to the Governor that he was writing: 26 October 1843. He was amazed that it was only a little over five years since he had arrived in the new colony, now known as Western Australia. So much had happened. It was already more than a year since he had been appointed Guardian of Juvenile Immigrants, receiving official notification only when the first batch of boys from the Parkhurst Reformatory on the Isle of Wright arrived at the colony. He did not yet know when more boys would arrive. He had hoped that the guardian's stipend would help him to clear his debts, but he had not cleared them all.

Schoales shivered and began to sort through his papers. There was so much to do, he wondered if he would ever get on top of it all. He picked up a bunch of papers and shuffled them until they made a neat bundle, and put them down under his paperweight – a rounded pink ballast stone that he had found on a beach during one of his trips to the south. He glanced again toward the window. On the wall beneath it was a large, grey mould stain, which had grown each winter for several years into the shape of *Terra Australis,* as shown on ancient maps. In a recent moment of frustration and depression, he had pencilled across it, in large letters, HERE BE DRAGONS.

He turned toward the door as he heard someone running toward it, and opened it before the visitor had time to knock. Chief Constable Hester stood on the step, in black oilskins. With his heavy moustache dripping-wet, he looked like a surfacing walrus. It seemed that this country made caricatures of them all – the sun shrivelled them, and the seasons mocked all their expectations.

'Come in out of the rain, Hester,' Schoales said.

Hester stamped and shook himself before stepping in,

but a puddle formed about his boots. 'I've just had word up from Fremantle, Mister Schoales.' The movement of his lips caused drops to fly from his moustache. 'A vessel has arrived in the Sound ... the *Shepherd*. She's gone aground trying to come round the wrong end of Rottnest Island. They've sent out boats, but it's a very heavy sea.' He drew breath. 'There's a batch of your lads on it.'

'Damn! I wasn't advised that they were coming,' he said. The *Shepherd* was the ship on which he had first come to the colony. He did not know then that the name was an omen, that he would become the shepherd of a flock. 'I'd better go down. I hope the lads aren't in danger.' It would be a tragedy if they were drowned at the end of such a long voyage, still-born at the end of those months in the foetid womb of a ship. 'I'll go down to Fremantle at once. You may like to walk with me, Hester, as far as the stables. I'm sure a brisk walk will warm you up.'

Schoales took an oilskin and a sou'-wester from the peg behind the door. As the rain had eased, he walked quickly with Hester to the livery stable, where his favourite mount was reserved for him; he had come to feel that he owned it.

He thanked Hester again and then mounted the horse. The familiar form of the saddle between his legs comforted him, as did the smell of freshly dressed leather, and the warmth of the horse against his calves. He did not mind the warm, pungent smells of horse manure and urine. He set out at a brisk pace along the track to Fremantle, which passed behind Mount Eliza, to meet the river again at Freshwater Bay, about halfway to the coast. He rested his horse for a while before continuing. The track led away from the river again, to skirt the high ground on the west of the bay.

The gale veered back to the west, bringing more rain. Raindrops and small hailstones stung his face. He bent his head, to take their force on the crown of his sou' wester, but water was forced inside his collar. Cold drops trickled down his chest and back. The sand was firmed by the rain, making it easier for his horse, and it broke into a trot to challenge the wind. He checked it, as there were stumps masked by the low scrub regrowth along the track. At least the rain had driven the kangaroos and wallabies into shelter and the horse would not be startled by one suddenly leaping from cover. Nor would there be snakes. Schoales had an Irishman's terror of snakes.

He made good time toward the coast, where the track turned south, seaward of the limestone hills known as the Seven Sisters, to reach the river just upstream from Fremantle, which was at the river's mouth. He stopped to scan the sea. The worst of the storm had moved inland and the thunder had diminished to a snarl behind him, but the rain-driven sea spray prevented any glimpse of the ship. Under the dark, angry sky, the grey tea-trees and dark-green native pines looked even harsher, denser and more sombre on the lower slopes.

At home, they sometimes had wild storms out of the Irish Sea, but there the rain was most often soft, not much more than mist, seldom driven like shot by gales.

He was glad to descend again into scrubby shelter where the track descended to the river. Fortunately, the ferry was waiting at the northern bank. It began its return journey as soon as he had coaxed his horse to board it. He held its head on a short rein, and kept talking quietly to it as the ferry battled with the wind and the incoming tide. The ferry berthed at the eastern end of the town, where the houses were scattered among bare dunes. Most of the trees and shrubs had been cut down and the wind whipped sand before it.

Leaving the horse at a stable, Schoales walked down High Street, the main street of the town, running westward to Arthur's Head, the southern head at the river mouth. Toward the Head, the houses and commercial buildings gathered together sociably; their limestone boundary walls – built to hold back the shifting sand – linked rather than separated them, hinting at urban order. The smaller limestone cottages reminded him of Irish farmhouses.

The rain had eased again, although the gale still blew, and the driven sand stung his face. The tide was high enough for the wind to drive sea water over the south end of Cliff Street, which crossed the end of High Street inside the Head. The signal flags and the Union Jack on a mast beside the Round House, the limestone-walled prison on the Head, snapped in the gale.

He climbed the stairs and went to the sea wall beyond the Round House, near the foot of the signal mast. Rain still obscured the view. Surf crashed on the rock bar that barred ships from entering the mouth of the river. Below him, in Bathers' Bay, whalers were struggling to set extra anchors. He turned back to the shelter of the Round House and accosted one of the Fremantle merchants.

'What's happening, Mister Bateman?' He had to shout; even in the shelter, the wind snatched the words from his mouth.

'The stupid master took the South Passage and struck a rock. She seems to be holding together. Boats went out some time ago and should be back soon … that looks like one now. They could've all been drowned.'

Through the haze of rain and spray, a sail could be seen – one of the local cutters that had been despatched to rescue the passengers. It surfed toward the shelter of the bay, south of the Head, under reefed sails. Schoales waited until it had rounded the point into calmer waters; it was too rough for it to come alongside the small jetty. He then hurried toward the beach and waited in the shelter of the hull of a ship, victim of an earlier storm.

The cutter came about into the wind, as close as it could safely approach the beach. Two men leapt overboard into water up to their midriffs. Each reached up to take a woman and carry her ashore. When the two bedraggled women were set on the beach, Schoales called them into the inadequate shelter of the wrecked hull. They wept hysterically. He joined the two men who plunged back into the shallows, and carried two small, terrified boys back to shore on his shoulders.

One of the juvenile immigrants, from the *Simon Taylor* batch, ran from the nearby Immigration Depot to see what was happening. Schoales instructed him to lead the group to the nearest inn. 'If there are other lads at the Depot, tell them to come to me.'

The next rescue boat was unloaded more quickly, as more

men arrived with the women and children. Within half an hour, two other boats arrived. There were cries of relief as families came together; others stood forlornly at the edge of the water, scanning the sea for other boats. Schoales asked one of the men to assist the lads who had been fetched, to take the passengers to shelter in homes and inns, and to begin listing their names and where they were to be quartered.

It was an hour before a boat came with some of the Parkhurst boys. They stared, white-faced, at the shore. The helmsman urged them to jump overboard, but none moved. A sailor picked up one boy and dropped him over the side. He came up spluttering and terrified, his head not much above the waves, and floundered toward the beach. Schoales rushed into the sea, dragged him to the beach and urged him into the shelter of the hull, then plunged back into the water, calling and waving to the remaining boys. Some jumped; others had to be dropped over the side by impatient sailors. Schoales and several of the men stood, thigh deep, where they could grab each boy, help him to his feet, and urge him toward the beach.

When all were ashore, Schoales returned to the hulk, the lower half of his body chilled. He supposed that some of the boys might have been in Thames hulks before the Parkhurst Reformatory was opened. They must have thought that they had been sent to another. He hastily counted the bewildered boys: thirteen, an ill-favoured number.

The wind shrieked through gaps in the rotting hull. He noticed one boy, more robust and self-possessed than the others. 'What's your name, lad?'

'Kirk ... John Kirk, sir!' His blue lips could hardly frame the sounds. He shivered violently.

'I'm your guardian here, Kirk ... Schoales. How many lads were there on the ship? Is everyone safe?'

'Twenty-eight, Mister Schoales.' His teeth chattered between each syllable. 'There'll be more in the next boat. I think they're all safe.'

'Good lad! I'll get someone to take you to the Depot while I wait for the rest.'

The rest of the boys arrived half an hour later, on another boat. As soon as they were all ashore, Schoales shepherded them from the exposed beach to the lee of stone walls and made them trot – for warmth as well as haste – to the Immigration Depot in the Customs House, a large, plain limestone building with a shingled roof further round the bay.

As soon as the door was shut behind them, the boys began to chatter loudly. The room was already steamy. The first batch of boys gathered nude before the fire, their clothes draped over ropes strung across one end of the room.

'Strip off,' Schoales instructed the second batch.

Some were unexpectedly modest and slow, but soon all but one were naked. How pale and wretched they looked, their genitals blue and wrinkled, like some of the baboons at Cape Town. Some had sores, some were pockmarked. They needed feeding for flesh, and sunshine for colour. Sea bathing would clean up their skins. Some of the boys were so frail and puny they looked scarcely twelve years old; two poor wretches apparently only infants. However, Schoales had learnt, with the first party that came on the *Simon Taylor*, that malnourishment may have retarded their development by three or four years. Several of those first arrivals were still quartered at the Depot, waiting to be assigned to new masters. Schoales asked one to bank up the fire, and another to tell the housekeeper to serve bread and soup. He was pleased to see these lads, after only a year of his guardianship, moving more confidently.

The room had become stuffy with steam and the stench of wet boys and dirty clothes. The smell would have been worse if they had not all had an involuntary dip in the sea. He noticed that some boys bore, besides other sores or pock-marks, scars and bruises – some fresh and possibly acquired on the rough trip from the stranded ship, but others older. One had a peculiarly shaped head; the forehead was narrow, but the back of his skull was disproportionately large, particularly on the right-hand side. He held his head, slightly tilted back, seemingly defiant, but the tilt may have been due to the deformity. Who would want to take on such an unprepossessing lad?

'What's your name, lad?'

'John Gavin.' The name sounded like one word: *Jongavin*. His voice was surly.

'Go closer to the fire. There'll be hot soup for you all soon.'

Schoales walked over to the boy who had not undressed. He was more puny and paler than the others, his hair so fair it might have been bleached. He crouched in a corner like a frightened animal. Schoales called over one of the *Simon Taylor* boys to help him, and they began to remove the boy's wet, filthy clothes. He did not resist. When he was naked, he crouched even lower and placed his hands over his head as if he expected a blow. There was a scar a few inches long on the left side of his throat, which was still red. Schoales wrapped him in a blanket and set him in a warmer place, then called over John Kirk and asked, 'Who's that lad? Is he ill?'

'Edward Robinson, sir.' Now warm and dry, Kirk was more confident. 'He's a mad'un. Tried to cut 'is throat with a blunt knife . . . and to drown 'imself.'

Schoales wondered if there was more to it than that. He would get a report from the *Shepherd*'s master later. He turned over a pile of clothes with his foot and told the boys to hang them on one of the ropes. The clothes were ragged, some boots split. He turned again to Kirk – the boy seemed intelligent and even had an air of petty authority.

'I suppose your other slops are still on board the *Shepherd*, Kirk.'

'We ain't got no others.'

'Damn! They should've sent you out with at least one spare set. Stocks are low here.' Schoales, as his trousers and boots began to steam, became more aware of the chill in the lower half of his body. 'We've too few mattresses, Kirk. You'll have to make do tonight with blankets on the floor. I'll make sure there's enough wood to keep the fire blazing overnight. I'll be back in the morning.'

The storm was abating when he left, but the wind still strong enough to intensify the chill of his damp clothes. He wrapped his oilskin tightly about himself, checked that his horse had been rubbed down and fed with oats, and then walked to an inn to take a room for the night. He asked for a meal to be sent to his room. While waiting for it, he stripped and dried himself, glad that a fire had been lit in the room. He hung his damp clothes on two chairs and set them to dry. He would have to begin finding masters for this new batch of lads.

When the innkeeper brought the meal, he had to wake Schoales.

2

In the following weeks, Schoales found masters for most of the new arrivals. He rode to Fremantle on the Wednesday before Christmas, as some of the lads were now working in the town and he must check on things at the Depot. Besides, it would be cooler near the sea. Even at the early hour, the still air was warm, so he rode slowly, taking time to look about him. Honeyeaters were busy among the blossoms of the trees, darting from bough to bough, from tree to tree. Several wallabies stood to watch him pass, their forearms held out submissively. The strange, stiff banksia flowers were loud with swarms of bees, and stands of hives were set in the scrub.

Some days, when the heat was intolerable, he hated the drab wiriness of the scrub. But in the spring, it became a glorious garden, a veritable Eden. Every twig, even those that had seemed dead at the end of summer, bore strange flowers, many fragile and delicate. Yet many people still thought that the Australian bush was an affront to nature.

The tide was not running, so the ferry crossed still water, although the surface was rippled by the first puff of the early sea breeze. The damp salt smell invigorated him. He booked a room for two nights at Francisco's inn, the Crown and Thistle – quite a decent inn, with a good table and palatable wines, some French. It was also a good place to meet merchants, ship owners and, occasionally, farmers down to the port on business – potential employers for the lads.

He found all in good order at the Depot; the housekeeper, Mrs Jenkins, was competent and the lads liked her. There were only three at the Depot – two were between assignments, the third was Edward Robinson.

'Young Edward's nervy,' Mrs Jenkins reported. 'But he's better now the other boys from the ship have gone. They teased him an awful lot. And he's keeping himself cleaner ... hasn't soiled his trousers for a week or more.'

'Thank you, Missus Jenkins. I'm sure your good care is a great help to him.'

'He's missing John Gavin though. They were thick as thieves.'

Schoales smiled at the apt, but possibly ill-chosen phrase.

'I hope Gavin's settling with the Pollards. They were the only ones who'd take him on.'

The Pollards were among the immigrants he had arranged passage for when he had gone to England as an immigration agent. Travelling with them back to the colony, he had admired the way the parents related to their children, instilling obedience with love and firmness.

'Maybe it's time to find a master for Robinson. I'll spend a little time with him tomorrow.'

Schoales had arranged to join a small group of merchants and professional men for lunch at the Crown and Thistle, but allowed himself time to walk around the shore of South Bay to Arthur's Head. He hoped that his friend, the Reverend George King, would be at his small Aboriginal school at the western end of the bay, but no one was there. He crossed the point, and walked on to the beach at Bathers' Bay. Aborigines, including the children from the little school, clustered around a whale carcass drawn up by the tryworks, and snatched at large chunks of flesh tossed to them by one of the whalers. He decided to bring young Robinson down in the morning; it might amuse him.

He walked through the Whalers' Tunnel under the Head, to return to the town, passing the empty stocks at the end of High Street. He paused near the blacksmith's shop at the corner of Cliff Street. The blacksmith was pounding a red-hot piece of iron with a heavy sledge. Between strokes, he nodded and Schoales raised a hand in acknowledgement before walking on to the hotel at the next corner.

He was the last to arrive at the dining room. One of the merchants, Jones, who had apprenticed one of the lads, welcomed him warmly.

'We don't see you often enough, Mister Schoales.'

'I've been busy finding work for the Parkhurst lads.'

'I'm satisfied with the boy you sent me. He's coming on well.' Jones turned to his neighbour at the table. 'I was just telling Mister Austin here, before you came in, that I'd look hard at forty pounds before I would lose him.'

'I'd be prepared to try one of your boys, Mister Schoales,' Austin said.

'On your vineyard, Mister Austin?'

'Some light work in the vineyard, but chores in the garden as well – chop wood, sweep and clean, that sort of thing.'

'All the available lads are taken, especially with the harvest under way. I have only one boy not yet spoken for, but rather

a sad case. He's too nervy for his own good. Other lads
bullied him during the voyage out. His condition was desperate on arrival and I asked the Governor to consider
committing him to medical supervision or sending him back
to Parkhurst. However, he's on the way to being settled now
that the other lads have left the Depot. Would you be prepared
to risk trying him?'

'I need to discuss it with my wife.'

'Of course! However, I'll not offer him to you until I'm
sure he's ready. Perhaps some time in the new year. I plan to
spend time with him tomorrow.'

'Are more boys coming?'

'Yes, but I don't know when, and I hope not too soon.
I now have forty-six to care for ... By the way, there are two
other boys. They're in the Round House, as they stole stores
on the voyage out. I believe they are contrite and may be
available soon.'

'Congratulations on the success of the scheme so far,'
Jones said.

'Not everyone agrees with you, but I believe the policy of
kindness with firmness will succeed,' Schoales said. 'I'm
working on some recommendations to His Excellency about
improvements. It takes so long to get approvals from the
Colonial Office back home.'

'What sort of things do you have in mind?' Austin asked.

'For one, I'm thinking of a small experimental farm, or a
botanical garden to test plants for acclimatisation ... something more ambitious than James Drummond's government
garden.'

'A good idea,' Jones said, nodding. 'We need to test new plants, crops and ornamentals.'

'Yes. We also need to know more about the indigenous plants. So far, we've not begun to use them, apart from some trees for timber. She-oak's good for shingles and jarrah's good for house and boat building, and excellent for furniture . . .'

Austin interrupted. 'They call it Swan River mahogany at home. I hear they are using blocks of it to pave some streets in London.'

'Yes,' Schoales said. 'However, such schemes have to be funded from home and the Colonial Office isn't generous. I'd be grateful if good accounts of the lads were sent to His Excellency.'

'I'll do that gladly,' Jones said.

Next morning, Schoales walked with Robinson to Arthur's Head. The boy refused to pass through the Whalers' Tunnel, even though it was short, and the white beach could be seen through the far opening. Schoales led the way across the dunes at the southern end of the Head. He pointed out the intricate patterns made in the windswept sand by the foot-prints of gulls. Schoales sat on the sea wall and suggested to the boy that he might find shells by the sea.

Robinson was reluctant to go at first, but began to be interested in the busy scene: whalers raking ash from under the trypots, repairing rigging, sharpening harpoons. After a while, he moved away slowly, like a rabbit from a burrow, testing the ground, and began to pick over shells lying among the brown ribbon weed just beyond the lap of the waves. Schoales was pleased to see that the boy did not retreat when one of the whalers called a loud but friendly greeting. He moved slowly toward the trypots, as if hypnotised by the activity. Schoales left him alone for half an hour and then called him. 'We must go back to the Depot, Edward. I wish to return to Perth.'

On the way back to the Depot, Schoales bought a small pocket-knife at a store, which he offered to Robinson.

'It's an early Christmas present, Edward, because you've been a good lad lately. I'll see you again after Christmas. I hope I'll found a kindly master for you.'

Schoales was glad to see that the boy smiled when he took the knife and opened and closed its blade.

'Be careful with it, lad. It's sharp.'

'Every boy needs one of those.'

Schoales turned to see who had spoken. A tall man, with a ruddy face and cheerful expression approached him and held out his hand to shake. 'Mister Schoales, isn't it?' he said. 'I'm Pomeroy.'

Schoales grasped his hand and said, 'I'm glad to meet you. You've taken up land near Bull's Creek, I hear.'

'That's right, although I plan to move to York after Easter. The land's better there. It's a bit lonely out at Bull's Creek, and my wife and I wondered if one of your Parkhurst boys might like to spend Christmas with us and our children. I've some work he could do . . . enough for a week or two. It would give me a chance to see how he gets on. Later, when I move to York, I might want to have him, or another of your boys, assigned to me.'

Pomeroy smiled at Robinson, who smiled back. Schoales

was pleased to see his quick response to Pomeroy's kindly manner. He patted Robinson on his head.

'There's only this lad, Edward, not yet assigned. Your offer may be a blessing. He was tormented by the other boys, and was in a bad way for a while ... but he's much better now, and if you only want him for a week or two, I see no risk of him causing you problems. It would do him a lot of good, I think, and give me a chance to see if he's ready for assignment. Thank you.' He turned to the boy. 'Edward, this kind man, Mister Pomeroy, has invited you for Christmas. Would you like that?'

The boy smiled and nodded. 'I'll bring my knife, in case I need it,' he said.

'Come with us then, Mister Pomeroy,' Schoales said. 'I'll introduce you to the housekeeper and you can make arrangements with her. I have to go back to Perth.'

3

On Christmas Eve, Schoales closed his office early and rode out to spend a few days with his sister Elizabeth and her husband, Richard Nash. They had built a home on their allotment beside the Swan River at Guildford. Since he was early, he rode leisurely.

The soil beside the upper reaches of the Swan was one of the few fertile tracts found so far in the sandy coastal plain. There were signs of the farmers flourishing. The harvests were in, the hay stooked, and bunches of grapes were swelling on regimented ranks of vines. A gentle sea breeze had come in early from the south-west, impregnated with fecund odours as it moved slowly over the drying hay and loamy soil. However, he knew, from his time as secretary of the York Agricultural Society, that too little good soil had been discovered.

Schoales was content to let the horse amble at its own pace. He let the reins lie loosely on its neck, freeing his hands to fondle its ears. He gently turned back its right ear and bent to speak into it. 'Save your energies, Samson. Richard plans a duck shoot on Boxing Day.' The horse, sensing excitement in Schoales's voice, whinnied and quickened its pace.

Elizabeth embraced him when he arrived, and then stood back. 'You look well, John,' she said. 'I was worried last time. You looked rather peaky. Richard's in the sitting room.'

The house was comfortably furnished and settled, while

some houses still had a temporary air. The walls of the sitting room had been freshly whitewashed, with a touch of pink in the wash. Two red druggets partially covered the jarrah floorboards, which had deepened with many applications of wax polish. The sofa under the front window was covered with green chintz, nearly the same colour as the curtains. Over the open fireplace was a new, heavy mantelpiece of jarrah, and between the fireplace and the window was a large mahogany chiffonier.

Nash and Schoales retreated to the parlour, which adjoined the sitting room and opened onto the veranda. Its large window commanded a view of the steep bank falling to the river.

'Things seem to be going well with the Parkhurst boys,' Nash said.

'I think so. It was hard to find masters for two of the second batch, but I have placed one – a difficult boy – with the Pollards at South Dandalup. I plan to visit them in a couple of weeks to check on the boy's progress. But there are problems, and I'm thinking about some proposals to present to the Governor.'

'Will Hutt agree?' Nash asked.

'I think so ... I've found him supportive generally. However, I'm not sure about the authorities at home – the Parkhurst people and the Colonial Office. It takes so long to get decisions ... and I don't think it's just because mail takes so long.'

'It took me a whole year, once, to get a reply to a letter,' Nash interjected.

'I don't think they understand our needs,' Schoales continued.

Nash nodded. 'Yes, they're too far away to appreciate our situation. You must be pleased, though, John. I hear good reports of some of your lads.'

'Yes, but there are more intractable lads among the second batch on the *Shepherd*. I've asked the Governor to request the Parkhurst people to send more information about each boy, especially their tempers ...'

'Are you coping with the demands of the job?'

'So far, but there's more to do than I expected, especially now that I've forty-six boys in my care. I have to bank half their wages and pay any fines they might incur, represent them in court if they get into trouble ... and pay their legal costs. I can't do as much law work as I'd like. I need that income, because I still have debt to clear.'

'I thought selling the machinery at the mill would've helped you to clear your debts,' Nash said.

'Not entirely, I'm sorry to say. If those damned wood-cutters hadn't charged so much for firewood ...'

'And the Governor wouldn't fix prices. He said they should be determined by demand. Anyhow there's plenty of law work,' Nash said. 'So, if at any time you want to give up being guardian for those boys, I could give you work.' He stood up. 'But, let's forget all that for a while. I've a new claret here, from Sandalford, John Septimus Roe's place, just up the river. I think it'll set a standard here.'

He went into the sitting room and returned with a

dark-green bottle and two glasses. Nash filled the glasses. The wine was deep red in colour.

'I meant to tell you, Gerald Lefroy'll join us in a duck shoot on Boxing Day,' said Nash.

'I missed him when I was last in York. He'd gone exploring for land to the north. He and his brother have nearly finished their year with Burgess on his York farm, and feel they can manage on their own now.'

'He's staying with the Roes,' Nash said. 'He seems to have become a popular visitor there, particularly with Sophie.'

'Sophie! She's only a girl. Wasn't she one of the first to be born in the colony in 1829? She must be only fourteen, and he's nine or ten years younger than me . . . about twenty-four.'

'Perhaps he feels he can wait. There aren't many single girls of his age.'

Schoales smiled. 'You're probably right.' He paused. 'There are even fewer of my age.'

Nash noticed a disconsolate note in Schoales's voice.

'Talking of the Roes,' he said, 'let's try their wine.' He picked up a glass. 'Here's to the future, John.'

They both savoured the wine and were quiet until Elizabeth called them in to supper.

After supper, Schoales and his sister sang duets and enjoyed Nash's unfeigned praise of their performance.

'My dears,' he said, standing to clap, 'I've never heard you in better voice.'

Neither sensed the little envy that underlay his praise. Nash had no doubt that Elizabeth loved him generously, but she also loved her brother deeply. The pang of envy passed quickly when Elizabeth, having kissed her brother lightly on his cheek, moved quickly to Richard, her eyes sharply focussed with pleasure and passion, and embraced him tightly.

Gerald Lefroy came soon after breakfast on Boxing Day. He had grown a sandy-coloured beard since Schoales had last seen him. His shaven upper lip looked even deeper. The two friends went duck-shooting upstream from the house, where there was good cover near deep water. Nash had decided not to join them.

As they walked along the riverbank, Schoales said, 'It's good to see you, Gerald. You look fit, I must say.'

'I ought to be. Up betimes and labouring all day in the fields. I think I must have been born to be a farmer. You know I was never much of a scholar.'

'Have you found a piece of land for yourself yet?'

'No, but I'm off again soon with a couple of other fellows. We're looking up north. Most of the good land around York has been taken up.' He stooped and picked up a handful of the red soil. He licked it.

'Ugh!' Schoales said. 'What are you doing?'

'Testing the soil. I seem to get a measure of it from the taste. I hear Richard's planning a vineyard on these flats.'

'Will this soil be suitable?' Schoales asked.

'For grapes, I can't say. I can only judge for crops.'

They had soon shot two ducks each, and sat in the deep shade of a paperbark beside the river to cool down.

'I've never heard the full story of that trip home you had a couple of years ago, before I came ... to enlist migrants,' Lefroy said.

'I thought that would set me up. Some settlers promised to employ the migrants. As a lawyer, I should've known better and asked for contracts. I also expected to be paid a bonus by the government for every migrant I brought to the colony. When I got to London, the home authorities told me that bonus schemes had been done away with, but that I could buy crown land at a discount.'

'That sounds alright.'

'It would've been if I'd had capital. In one way, the trip was successful. I brought back about one-hundred migrants. But some of the farmers reneged on their promises, and I was saddled with the cost of maintaining some migrants until they were employed. I could not afford to take up the land offer. Eventually the Governor agreed to meet the costs of the unemployed migrants, but I had to surrender most of what I expected from the scheme.'

'I heard several people claimed that you'd lost money on their investments.'

'Several parents gave me money to invest on behalf of their sons who were migrating. One lot was for buying stock, but I maintain I was free to use my judgement with the others. Goods were scarce in the colony, so I invested some money in goods to sell. Unfortunately, two other vessels arrived at the same time as our ship, and prices fell ...'

They heard Elizabeth call from a distance, and began to

walk back to the house. Schoales slung the pair of ducks over his shoulder.

'What's this I hear about you and young Sophie Roe?' Schoales asked.

Lefroy grinned. 'I think she's fond of me. She's a beautiful young girl, and I'm prepared to wait a few years. Some say that girls mature more quickly here. Perhaps it's the climate.'

'Or maybe the freer life,' Schoales said.

'However, I have rivals, young de Burgh especially,' Lefroy said. 'And you?'

Schoales shifted the ducks to the other shoulder before he replied. 'Well I won't be a rival for you over Sophie.'

'There must be other young ladies,' Lefroy said.

Schoales shrugged. 'Nearly all of them are married.'

'None of them come anywhere near your sister,' Lefroy said.

Schoales nodded.

4

Mrs Pollard bustled in her kitchen. Although this first week of January had been very hot, she was glad to be preparing a meal for a visitor. The farm was not far from the new inland track through Pinjarra, but few went out of their way to visit, especially during the hot summers. Even their employer, Magistrate Singleton, did not come often from his main holding, which was some twenty miles away, although the Reverend Mr Wollaston had called twice, when on circuit, to catechise the children. However, Mr Schoales wrote that he was anxious to see how John Gavin was settling. She glanced at the clock and went to call Jane in from the dairy where she was setting the milk to separate.

When her daughter arrived, she thought how well she looked, becoming plumper, ripening in the heat like the melons in the pasture. She was likely to be comely, but of tender spirit, and a hard country is hard on tender spirits. She would make a good wife for some man. If only Mr Schoales was not different in class and age.

'Jane dear, don't forget that Mister Schoales will be here soon. We should bathe. You first. Wear the nice muslin.'

'Of course, Mam! I'd not forgotten.' She blushed with pleasure.

'Afterward, please fetch Pa and the boys, and choose some songs for tonight.'

After she had called in the others, Jane tried to busy herself, fussing with sprays of golden flowers from a late-blooming Christmas tree that she had put in a vase. On the plain wooden table, they glowed like flames in the darkening room.

The baby, Charles, whimpered in his parents' bedroom. He was wasted with heat and a fever, mild but lingering. Mrs Pollard turned anxiously at the cry.

'Watch the soup please, Jane. I must see to Charlie. It's thick, as Mister Schoales likes it, and it'll catch if you don't watch it.'

Jane was glad to have her attention directed. Her mother picked up a wet cloth that she had set to cool on the window ledge, and took it to the bedroom to bathe the hot forehead of her pale, thin baby. His cheeks had bright red medallions of fever flush.

Schoales looked forward to stopping for the night with the Pollards. He enjoyed the boisterous company of children, and their house was one of the few where he felt at ease. In other houses, he was often uncomfortable to be a bachelor when so many men of his age and station were married. The Pollards were two days riding from Perth and it was too long since he had seen them.

The track meandered through the scrub beside the South Dandalup River, an upper tributary of the Murray. At this season, it was reduced to a series of disconnected pools and reed beds beset by dense stands of paperbark trees, which reminded him of the convoluted trees on his sister's willow-pattern china. The stench of rot rose from the drying mud.

The track opened suddenly into a small clearing in which the house and farm buildings clustered about fifty yards from the bank of the river. The partly cleared pastures and a small wheat field lay beyond them, in the fertile soil contained within a large meander of the river.

The stubble in the recently harvested wheat field had the colour of pale madeira in the late-afternoon light; the standing stooks of hay cast long shadows. Schoales reined in his horse and stayed within the shadow of the trees to enjoy the scene. An evening such as this, with the late light gilding the scene, and the air cooled by a wind from the south, almost reconciled him to the fierce heat of a summer day. A large flock of black cockatoos, noisily repeating their cry, 'koorark, koorark', wheeled over the clearing, selecting a tree for their night's roosting.

The mud-brick house was whitewashed; white flakes, fallen on the ground, were so like snow he was surprised they did not melt. A lean-to of slabs had been added at the rear to accommodate the family. The carpenter's shop, beyond the house, was made of jarrah slabs, bleached grey in a few summers. Anyone fresh to the colony, remembering farm-houses at home, might think the buildings were ramshackle and decaying, but the stooked hay and the cattle in the pasture were signs that the farm might survive and prosper in time.

He had been frank with John Pollard, that the *Shepherd* boys were more fractious than those of the *Simon Taylor*. The report from the ship's master listed Gavin as one of a small rebellious gang, but not the ringleader. He appeared not to have joined the others in stealing stores during the voyage and he had, with Robinson, given evidence against the others at the inquiry into the thefts.

He looked back toward the house. The sun dipped behind clouds and the light reddened. For a moment, the stooks looked as if they were aflame and he felt an odd foreboding; there had been too many tragic fires.

'We'll both eat and rest well tonight, Samson,' he said, fondling the ears of his horse.

The horse whinnied and set off at a fast walk toward the homestead. Schoales steered him to the stables, where George, the eldest son, was filling a manger in preparation for his arrival. He left the horse with him and went to wash at the enamel bowl on the tank stand near the corner of the stables.

When he entered the kitchen, Jane was standing by the fireplace, stirring whatever was cooking in a cauldron suspended over the fire. She did not hear him, and he did not speak. A shaft of late light through the window picked out lights in her thick brown hair. He was surprised to see how much she had grown since he had last seen her, in the winter – not so much in height as in fullness.

'Good evening, Jane.'

She dropped the spoon into the soup and stepped back quickly to avoid splashing drops.

'Bother!' She blushed with confusion. 'You startled me,' she said.

He crossed the room to her side, took a toasting fork from its hook and extricated the spoon. He smelt her freshness, conscious that his own ablutions had been perfunctory.

'There, Jane!' He held up the spoon. 'I'm sorry I startled you. Have you a cloth I can wipe this with?'

Mrs Pollard, entering from the bedroom, smiled when she saw them there, heads bent to a small task. Charles had finally gone to sleep.

'How nice to see you, Mister Schoales. You're in good time.'

'It's good to be here. It's been a long day.'

'John and the boys will be in soon ... and John Gavin. They are always glad to see you.'

'How's Gavin getting on?'

'Well enough with John and the boys. He's thick with George, but ...' She glanced away. 'You must be thirsty after your ride. Jane, bring Mister Schoales cool water from the filter.'

'I'm glad you agreed to give Gavin a chance,' Schoales said. 'No one else would. I did warn you that he might be difficult. Have *you* had any trouble?'

'Sometimes he's disobedient, and he sulks if I scold him.'

'It's enough for you to complain. I'll talk to him.'

'What worries me more is the way he looks. It disturbs me, that strange head.'

She was interrupted by the arrival of her husband, a stocky, grizzled man. The years as a linen-worker in Dublin had not entirely erased the weathered lines and colour of his face, acquired in his years in the navy. Schoales knew that he was about fifty, but he brought a gusty vigour into the kitchen, making it seem overcrowded. His sons, George, Thomas and Michael, followed him. They crowded around Schoales to welcome him and then clamoured for food.

'Manners!' Their mother spoke firmly. 'Have you all washed? Tommy ... there's still a tidemark on your neck ... go and wash properly. Sit down here, Mister Schoales ... George, help Jane with the soup. Where's John Gavin?'

'He's comin', Mam,' said Michael. 'When he heard Mister Schoales was comin', he went to change his shirt.'

'Well! I'm surprised that he sets an example in some things, and do say com*ing*. Mister Schoales won't like such rough talk.'

Gavin came in quietly and unnoticed while the others chattered. Schoales was relieved to see that he had a healthier colour and was carrying a bit more flesh on his thin frame. He also seemed less truculent and suspicious.

'You look well, John,' Schoales said. 'Missus Pollard obviously feeds you well. She tells me that you're getting on. We'll have a chat later, but, since you've made progress, here's a small reward.'

Gavin walked toward him. Schoales was sad to see that his misshapen head would never allow him to move with grace. He handed Gavin a small pocket-knife, which Gavin grasped quickly and turned to show George.

'Sit down, boy. Next to Michael.' Mr Pollard's voice was gruff, but Schoales was pleased that its tone was kindly. 'The boy never gets tired of my stories about Trafalgar, Mister Schoales.'

Pollard, as a young seaman on the *Victory*, had witnessed the death of Nelson; he still spoke of this with bated breath on each Trafalgar Day.

'My husband enjoys having a fresh audience for his tales, Mister Schoales,' Mrs Pollard said, smiling.

'By the way, do call me John, please. We're old friends now,' Schoales said.

'Thank you then, John. It's a bit confusing ... three Johns at the one table.'

The news-hungry family showered Schoales with questions about Albany and the Vasse as well as about Perth. Most of the news was of interest to Mr Pollard and the boys; Mrs Pollard hungered for feminine things. Schoales also brought overseas news, already more than half a year old by the time it reached the colony, a few weeks older still by the time he carried it to Dandalup. He enjoyed the free talk in which there was no affectation. Too many in the colony strove for a gentility that life here could barely support yet.

After the soup, there was a haunch of kangaroo, baked with herbs. Some families had banished kangaroo meat from their tables once their stock began to multiply, but Schoales did not think that it was inferior to venison. And he understood that the Pollards' days were full of grinding tasks, and it would be years before they could be sure of anything beyond survival. However, it might not be better for them at home now, where unemployment was rising.

'The news from England's not good. Many are out of work, especially in Liverpool.'

The Pollards were living in Liverpool when Schoales selected them for immigration.

'Well, thank goodness we took up your offer, Mister Sch ... John.'

'There's more trouble at home, in Ireland. O'Connell's been agitating again.'

'It's good to be away from that strife, too,' Pollard said.

'I'd also hoped we'd be free of religious contention here,' Schoales said. 'But the papists have been stirred up by the visit of Father Brady ... I'd hoped that, here, we'd make a clean break from all that.'

As soon as the meal was finished and cleared away, the family called upon Schoales to sing to the accompaniment of Jane on a small, worn harmonium. He sang them some senti- mental Irish ballads, and a rousing hymn or two. He called on Jane to join him in some duets. Her voice was untrained, not always true, but touching in its hesitant and gentle striving.

Standing close to her, he studied her while he turned the pages. She was not pretty, but her grey eyes were flecked with candlelight, and her face had a pleasing animation, its bones starting to set in their adult mould. He guessed that such bones would support the flesh against early sagging; she would be a handsome matron if life treated her well. Her complexion was not yet withered by the sun and dry winds, but a harsh life might lie ahead of her. He was unexpectedly touched by her nearness, touched without any of that nervous fibrillation he sometimes felt when singing duets with Mrs Symmons at her dinner parties, or in the choir.

Now that the fire had been allowed to die down, the only light came from the candles on the two brackets on the harmonium. Only Jane and Schoales were within the sphere of their immediate light; the others were dimly lit. Mrs Pollard watched Schoales and her daughter, knowing that they could not see her watching. Schoales's face was narrow, lightly tanned after several days riding, framed by dark, wavy hair. She sighed.

A log fell on the embers in the fireplace, briefly stirring a bright flame. Jane's white muslin dress seemed to catch fire momentarily.

5

Schoales returned by easy stages from the Pollards, calling at other farms. In general, his lads were going well, but nothing pleased him more than Gavin's settling with the Pollards, who were strict but kindly. He had accepted an invitation to visit the family again at Easter.

He returned to his desk refreshed and buoyed, dealt with his papers with more despatch, and wrote a memo to the Governor announcing that the Parkhurst scheme promised success, but proposing amendments to improve it:

However, it is well known that many looked with jealousy on the arrival of these lads, and were neither slow to avow nor gentle in their mode of expressing their determination to prevent if possible the introduction of what they were pleased to determine convicts. Yet now I believe it would be difficult to find one who would point out evil arising from the system or deny its good practical effects.

By late January, Schoales was confident that Edward Robinson was stable. He had behaved well with Pomeroy and had been reluctant to leave when his short assignment ended, because the Pomeroys were preparing to move to York. He had not reverted to dirty habits when he returned to the Depot.

To test him, Schoales asked the boy to accompany him on a walk, and deliberately left him to fend for himself in High Street, slipping away while the lad was engrossed in watching the harnessing of a horse-team. Schoales followed him discreetly, and was elated when Robinson found his own way back to the Depot and showed no distress.

On the following day, when he had returned to his office, Schoales wrote to Austin, offering him Robinson, as Pomeroy would not be ready to accept him yet. He was pleased that Austin replied within a few days, agreeing to accept the lad by mid-February. He enjoyed drafting a short memo to the Governor:

... at that time, there was strong ground to doubt his sanity and his memory was wretched and a sharp question or a hasty order completely discomposed him. After some weeks my attention was drawn to him most particularly and I perceived that, removed from the annoyance of the other lads who made him their butt, he was rapidly improving ... I believe I have found a kind and considerate master in J. Austin whose method with the boy together with the kindness of his lady, have greatly pleased me.

Someone knocked at the door gently. Schoales opened the door and was surprised to see Mrs Symmons. She was dressed in riding habit, which enhanced the slenderness of her waist. Her horse was hitched to a rail of the fence.

'Missus Symmons!'

'I was passing, Mister Schoales. We missed you at Saint George's on Sunday.'

Schoales sang in the choir at the church with Mrs Symmons and her husband, as well as Richard and Elizabeth.

'I was called away to deal with a problem with one of the boys.'

'Charles gets called away often now, since he became Protector of the natives,' Mrs Symmons said.

Schoales had heard criticism of Charles Symmons, that he saw himself as the punisher rather than the protector of the natives.

'He's away now.' Mrs Symmons pouted and patted her calf with her riding crop.

Schoales wondered if it was an impatient or nervous gesture. As it was a warm day, there was a dew of perspiration on her forehead and on the fine, pale down of her upper lip. The scent of perspiration blended provocatively with that of lavender water.

'May I come in?'

Schoales opened the door more widely and beckoned her in.

'I was passing,' she said, 'so I thought I'd call and see if you are free tonight. I've a few people coming for dinner. It will be a musical evening. I thought that we might sing that duet again.' She reached out and grasped his upper arm and looked at him beseechingly. 'Please do come.'

Schoales flinched at her touch – not from pain, but from the promise of a pleasure he must deny himself. He noticed a small patch of white powder on her cheek, but suppressed an urge to take out his handkerchief and wipe it away.

Schoales hesitated before refusing. He had a lonely evening ahead of him, but he felt that he might be compromised if he visited Mrs Symmons when her husband was away.

'Thank you,' he said, 'but I ... I'm already engaged.'

Mrs Symmons pouted again. 'I'm disappointed,' she said. 'I hope you'll be free next time.'

She turned away and walked out the door. Her scent lingered as Schoales watched her. With her riding crop, she slashed at a flower on a shrub beside the path. He longed to call her back.

Mrs Symmons did not look back as she mounted her horse. Schoales became aware of a pain in his hand. He was gripping the door handle too tightly.

6

With all the boys from the *Shepherd* now assigned to masters, Schoales found time, during the remainder of January, to take more law work. They were mostly petty cases but they gave him some much-needed extra income. The last, on the second day of February, was to defend a workman charged with theft. On his way to the Courthouse, he met Singleton, the magistrate from Pinjarra, who greeted him warmly.

'I was down your way recently, Singleton,' Schoales said. 'I stayed overnight with the Pollards, tenants of yours. A good family.'

'You've not heard?'

'Heard what?'

'A sad and terrible business ... the family's devastated, especially Missus Pollard.'

'Tell me. It's not anything to do with John Gavin, I hope, the Parkhurst boy they took on.'

'No. It was their daughter Jane.'

'Jane! Is she ill?'

'No. She's dead.'

Singleton noticed that Schoales blanched. He knew that he was friendly with the Pollards, and regretted breaking the news so abruptly.

'How?'

'A terrible accident ... she was burnt ... and I had to enquire into it. That wasn't easy. Missus Pollard was hysterical.

The kitchen fire must have flared and caught her ... Jane's dress. She ran out of the kitchen but fell into dry stooks.'

Schoales remembered the stooks touched by the red light of sunset, appearing to be afire. He remembered the family gathered at the table, the singing afterward, and Jane softly lit by candlelight and fire glow.

'My God! How awful ... a sweet young girl. We sang together. Awful ... did she suffer?'

'Not for too long, blessedly. The burns were serious. I'm sorry to have been the bearer of the news. I thought you might have heard.' He pulled out his watch and looked at it. 'I'm afraid I'm due in court, will you excuse me.'

'I too. I'll walk with you.'

The case was dealt with quickly, and Schoales returned to his office where he sat a while, still shaken by the news. He remembered how the light of the fire had enhanced Jane's face. That evening had promised so much for the family, and he had come away satisfied with Gavin's progress. Mrs Pollard, especially, would be shattered; her daughter was obviously her favourite child.

He got up suddenly and took his broad-brimmed hat from the peg behind the door. After standing a while on the step – hat in hand and undecided – he walked a few paces, stopped and turned back. He picked up his riding crop from the top of the dusty cupboard and strode off toward the town. But he turned up Mill Street and left into Saint George's Terrace. He failed to acknowledge the greetings of a few acquaintances, who wondered at his unusual incivility.

At the end of the Terrace, he cut left through the bush and followed a worn track toward the top of Mount Eliza. A small pack of stray dogs, in readiness for which he had brought the crop, bailed him up. He thrashed out at them with unusual viciousness until they retreated, yelping and snarling. He was momentarily ashamed of the pleasure he took in their pain before he strode on quickly, soon perspiring. On his way, he slashed at spider webs and the shrubs with his crop.

Near the crest, on the edge of the bluff, he dropped to the ground in the shade of a clump of she-oaks and welcomed the weak easterly, cooled by its passage over the water. When he had recovered his breath, he walked on slowly along the edge of the bluff, as far as a popular viewing point above the steam mill. No smoke came from its chimney, as the season's grain had now all been ground.

Near the mill, the river narrowed between two wide reaches: Perth Water to the left, in front of the town, and the much larger Melville Water downstream to the right. The river was estuarine as far as Perth. Shenton's windmill stood on the other side of The Narrows, the wind too light to turn its sails.

Schoales sat down with his back against a tree. There were few sounds – even the birds were quiet in the heat of the day. The town was hidden here by part of the bluff to the left. Apart from the two mills, there was little to show the presence of civilising hands. A lighter, its crew labouring with oars to supplement the wind that barely swelled its sails, moved slowly upstream and passed beyond his view. He took no comfort from the idyllic scene and wondered if it would be intrusive to see the Pollards again so soon.

He stayed there an hour, partly dozing, stewing in the humid heat.

When he walked back, he was pleased that the pack of dogs recognised him and slunk away into the scrub before he could lash them again.

7

For the next few days, Schoales busied himself with the affairs of his wards. Now that he had forty-six boys under his care, he was called away more often. The paperwork accumulated alarmingly while he was away, and he had much to catch up with. He had not regained the ease of spirit he had enjoyed before Singleton brought the terrible news of Jane Pollard's death, and he looked forward to visiting his sister Elizabeth, who had written to him as soon as she heard of Jane's death, to invite him for the weekend.

By Friday afternoon, he had dealt with all his reports, and was glad to set aside the troublesome account books. He set off for his sister's house.

Roses were heavy with blooms in Elizabeth's garden, and the evening air was rich with a mix of floral perfumes and herbal scents. Elizabeth met him at the door and, after kissing him warmly, stepped back to survey him.

'You must have been shocked by the tragic news,' she said. 'And you've had so much else on your mind. Try and put your worries aside for the next two days.'

Schoales patted his sister's cheek. 'It was a shock, I admit.' He glanced away. 'But I'm beginning to get on top of things ... other things, I mean.'

'Good! I've heard some complain they don't see you so

much now and miss your singing at their musical evenings. Missus Symmons especially.'

He was glad that the red glare of the evening sky was behind him; Elizabeth would not notice that he had blushed.

'Enough of all that now, John. Richard's in the parlour. He has some more new wine for you to try,' Elizabeth said, turning toward the kitchen.

Schoales found the kitchen a cheerful place. The blue-and-white willow-pattern service was a pleasing touch of fantasy on the pine dresser. Here, the whitewash had been warmed with a touch of ochre, so that the walls glowed subtly where light fell on them. Since his last visit, Elizabeth had put up new checked gingham curtains in the same colour as the china service. He should get her to make some to brighten up his sparsely furnished bachelor's quarters. He offered to set the table.

'No. Go on through to Richard. We'll eat in the parlour,' she said. 'It'll be cooler there in this weather.'

Schoales passed into the parlour and found that Nash had gone out onto the veranda, which was high enough to be a balcony, because of the fall of the land toward the river. Bead curtains, put up to keep out flies and mosquitoes, clicked gently in the strengthening wind. The house was on a spur of high ground inside a tight meander of the river, which was shoaly here toward the end of summer. The Darling Range to the east merged into the darkening sky. Ducks and other waterfowl called from the reed beds in the shallows. Some ducks and black swans fed in a backwater. The swans' white wing-feathers flashed as they thrust their red beaks and long necks deep into the water. The ducks bobbed more rapidly in the shallows, reminding Schoales of machinery at one of the textile factories he had visited in England.

Nash, who was standing at the railing, turned and nodded to him. 'That was a terrible business about the Pollard girl.'

'Yes, awful,' Schoales said. 'I thought of calling on them at Easter, but I think it better not to go so soon.'

'Any good news?' Nash asked.

'I'm glad to say that all the lads are now assigned, except for one or two at the Fremantle Depot between assignments. I've even placed the two lads who were sent to the Round House for theft on the ship. They've served their time and seem genuinely contrite.'

'From what you told me about the way they organised the robbery, they must have some spirit.'

'I agree,' Schoales said. 'Good masters might make good servants of them. I've also placed that lad, Robinson.'

'The one who kept fouling his clothes?'

'Yes. I feel more relaxed than I have about my charges for some time, although those that came on the *Shepherd* have, in general, been longer in crime than the earlier batch. Some seem incorrigible. I've been called away more often than I expected, to deal with problems that some masters have had with lads assigned to them.'

'I know. Some of your friends complain that they haven't seen you lately. They've missed you from the choir at Saint George's.'

'I'm sorry about that. I reckon the demands on me are about four times more since the arrival of the second batch, and they're more widely spread over an area about the size of two Irish counties.'

'Come on, you two,' Elizabeth called. 'Before the soup gets cold.'

'I hope, John,' she said, as they joined her at the table, 'that you won't talk about your work all weekend.'

Nash, who had gone to the sideboard to open a bottle of wine, said, 'What do you make of the visit of Father Brady. I'm told he was sent from Sydney to see whether the Romans here need priests. There's even talk of bringing out some monks as missionaries.'

'George King rose to the bait,' Schoales said. 'You know how much he dislikes the Romans. I hoped we could leave all that behind in Ireland.'

'I agree with John,' Elizabeth said. 'We don't want all that disputation here. But, enough! I'll only set you both off again.'

Richard bent and kissed her on the cheek. 'You're right, my dear!' He poured wine into her glass. 'I really think that this colony's going to have excellent wines. Perhaps they'll mellow all of us.'

He moved to serve wine to Schoales. 'This is more of the Roe claret,' he said. 'It's an earlier vintage. Let's see how it's progressing.'

'Talking of the Roes,' Elizabeth said, 'your friend Gerald Lefroy's always calling on them, whenever he's down from York. He thinks he's making progress with his courtship.'

Nash sniffed the wine and sipped it. 'Coming along nicely. Those who know say that the climate and the soil here, along the Swan, are like those in parts of France. I'll definitely put in some vines on that lower ground.'

He gestured toward the window with glass in hand. Then he held the glass against the hanging lamp. 'Just look at the colour. Come, taste it in a toast . . . the Queen.'

Schoales and his sister raised their glasses. On an impulse, Richard walked through to the veranda and leant over the railing. 'Another toast. No, a libation this time.' He poured a little wine onto the soil below. At the outer reach of the lamplight, it had the colour of blood. He stepped back into the room. 'The blushful Hippocrene, eh?'

His full, smooth cheeks, framed by dark mutton-chop whiskers, flushed with pleasure as well as wine. Schoales laughed at how Bacchanalian he looked, with his curly dark hair. The happy sound delighted his sister.

'Do you know, Richard,' he said, 'I think the next generation here might be pagans.'

'Better than papists!'

Elizabeth admonished him. Richard reached along the table and gripped John's arm. 'John! Now you've got that scheme for the Parkhurst boys well launched, why don't you let someone else take over? You know there's more business than I can handle in my practice.'

'I'd begun to think of handing over, but I'll wait and see how the Governor responds to my memorandum.'

Schoales slept better that night, and was late rising in the morning. Although he said little during breakfast, Elizabeth was pleased to see that he appeared more relaxed, as if he were closer to deciding whether or not to continue as Guardian. Afterward, Nash diverted him by showing him the work in hand on the river-flat vineyard. In the afternoon they went to a neighbour's farm where a flock of emus were damaging the crops. They assisted the neighbour to shoot some of the flock and to drive the remainder well into the bushlands. Nash was also pleased to observe that Schoales appeared more decisive.

Schoales returned to the mill early on Monday morning, refreshed and ready to finish catching up with deskwork. In particular, over the next two weeks, he spent time developing his plans for improving the juvenile immigrant scheme. He redrafted a long memorandum to the Governor, several times. He incorporated changes as suggested by Nash and some other leading citizens. In general, they supported the proposals.

He also checked the journal in which he accounted for moneys earned by his lads that he had to deposit with the Western Australian Bank. John Kirk, for one, claimed that he was owed some money. He was sure that he would sort it out. If not, he would seek the help of one of the traders more skilled in accounting.

8

Mrs Pollard tossed in her sleep, tormented by a nightmare of Jane running screaming from the house, her dress in flames. Each nightmare ended with an image of her charred body in the ashes, hawks swooping for insects in the rising smoke, black cockatoos wheeling, calling loudly in alarm, the red feathers like fire in their tails.

Although it was barely a month since the tragedy, her hair had greyed noticeably, and drooping lines had set at the corner of her mouth. She had not smiled in that month. She felt, as she tried to stand, that a great weight oppressed her. Charles was crying, so she pulled on a dressing gown and went over to pick him up. She opened her nightgown to offer him her breast, although her milk was beginning to fail. She had stood one night, after John left, before the cracked mirror, beating her drying breasts in desperation. It was no wonder that Charlie did not thrive.

She wished that John was home, but he needed to take any temporary work on offer. She took a pencil and crossed another day on the almanac, and realised that it was 21 February, Ash Wednesday, and John would not return for another two days.

Surely, she had already sacrificed more than enough for Lent. Yet she must take some notice of the day or the boys would drift even further toward heathen ways. She had mislaid the small Bible that Mr Wollaston had left with them, but she still had the prayer book.

As she finished dressing, she heard a noise and went to the kitchen. John Gavin was standing there.

'What are you doing here? Call the others for breakfast.'

She undressed Charles and laid him in a basin of tepid water, splashing the water on his brow as if she were baptising him. Would the Reverend Wollaston come again in time to do so? She laid him in the cradle again, naked, and moved it to a cooler corner of the bedroom, and then went to the kitchen door. She stood on the step and sniffed the air. Her fear of fire was now obsessive, greater than her fear of snakes or of the blacks who came less often. After a fire, last year, on the other side of the river, flakes of ash fell like begrimed snow on the house and ground about it. A strong sea breeze had whisked away the ashes of the fire in which Jane died.

Her sons came toward her, dishevelled from their own restless sleeps on a hot night. She had planned to read from the prayer book, but the boys clamoured for food. She cut thick slices of bread for them to eat with honeycomb. There was no milk for their tea; there was too little fodder for the cows, and she kept the little they yielded for Charles.

'Where's John Gavin?' She could not bear the sight of him now, blaming him for the blight that had fallen on her family.

'I'm here.'

The boy often appeared with uncanny quietness. He always watched her in a way that troubled her, possibly because his misshapen head often listed to one side. She resolved to write to Mr Schoales that very night, to ask him to find another place for him. She thought that they had done enough for the boy, and there was less work for him now the boys were taking on more tasks.

'George, have you told everyone what's to be done today?'

'Yes, Mam! I'll be repairin' the fences down at the yard. Tommy'll take the cattle across the river for some green pickin's. Michael and John'll help me with the fence.'

'I'll put up some lunch for you, Tommy. Don't forget to take water and look out for fire. If you see any, let the cattle fend for themselves. You come back across the river straight away. The rest of you can come up here for lunch.'

When the boys had gone, she steeled herself to undertake the task of packing away Jane's few relics. Firstly, she took the dress that Jane had worn when she had sung with John Schoales, inserting dried lavender heads as she folded it carefully. There were not many things; so much of her clothing was worn and faded with much washing, but she could not bear to make cleaning rags of them. A string of glass beads, an old rag doll, a tortoiseshell comb with several broken teeth, a few ribbons. There was little else, but the task took longer than expected. When it was done at last, she took Charlie down to the river's edge where the slight breeze would soothe them both in the shade. She took the prayer book with her and did not take the direct path, as it led past the patch of blackened ground.

'Dear God!' she muttered, as she laid Charlie on the ground. It was as close to an oath as to a prayer.

She opened the prayer book and began to read one of the collects for Ash Wednesday:

Almighty and everlasting God, who hatest nothing thou hast made, and dost forgive the sins of all them that are penitent; create and make in us new and contrite hearts, that we, worthily lamenting our sins, and acknowledging our wretchedness . . .

In a fit of anger, because there was no comfort in the collect, she flung the prayer book toward the river. It fell into muddy ooze and sank slowly. She was overcome again with her leaden weariness, and leant against a tree. She fell swiftly, deeply asleep, and stayed so until Charles's fretfulness woke her again. She rose as if she had to wrench her limbs from the earth, and walked slowly to the house to prepare lunch for the boys. However, she was exhausted and lay down on her bed.

'Mam! Are you alright, Mam?' George shook her shoulder gently.

She looked up at him, hoping at first that it would be her husband. When his father was away, George seemed older, by his awareness of responsibility, and became her other rock. She thanked God that he was strong and healthy. He looked worried, though. Was it for her, or was he grieving for his sister?

'I feel poorly, George. I feel heavy, especially here.' She touched her chest and wondered why her empty breasts felt so heavy. 'A terrible weight. Help me up.'

George helped her to sit up and ease her legs over the edge of the bed, then supported her as she stood. They walked slowly toward the kitchen.

'There's a stew for lunch,' she said. 'Call the others.'

'I have, they'll be here soon,' George said.

Gavin opened the door and came inside, slamming the door behind him.

Mrs Pollard shrieked at him, 'You're forever slamming doors! That's the second time today I've told you. You never learn.'

George was alarmed by his mother's quick rage. He spoke sharply to Gavin. 'You'd better fetch that gimlet from the carpenter's shop before you have lunch.'

When the boys had finished their meal, Mrs Pollard responded to George's pleas, and allowed him to help her to bed, where she slumped down. She went to sleep immediately, as if she had swooned. George studied her anxiously for a while, and then covered her with a sheet. So that the baby would not disturb her, he moved the cradle into the coolest part of the kitchen. Gavin and Michael lingered at the table.

'John! Pick up that loose straw by the house and take it down to the cowshed.'

When Gavin had gone, George spoke to Michael. 'Clear the table and go back to fencin' with John. I'll wash the dishes, and then stay here for a while in my room. I'm worried about Mam . . . she's not well.'

Nearly an hour later, Mrs Pollard woke suddenly to find Gavin standing at the entrance to her bedroom, with a thick board in his hand. She felt that he was threatening her and pulled the sheet to her throat instinctively. 'What do you want, boy? Don't come in here without knocking.'

'I did, ma'am, but you was asleep.'

'Well! What do you want? Why aren't you working with George?'

Gavin hesitated and then said, 'I was workin' but George sent me ... 'e sent me with this bit of board what's broke off a door.'

'Leave it! Leave it, then! Leave it until your master comes.'

'When'll that be?'

'The day aft –' She broke off, and then said, 'Tonight!'

Gavin left. She lay back and slept again. She woke, not sure if she had heard, or dreamt that she had, someone singing in George's room on the other side of the wall. The words were clear: 'And when we close those gates again, we will be all true blue ...' She recognised the lines from a hymn that George had sung the previous evening. It was in a book that he had borrowed from a neighbour, a book of Orange songs. She lay back again, still dazed by sleeping in the heat of the afternoon, and fell back asleep. When she woke, she was not sure how long she had slept. Gavin had said that he had been working with George, so George must have got up. Who had been singing then? She felt troubled, and rose from the bed.

She found Gavin in the kitchen, drinking from a small basin. 'What are you doing here?' she screeched. 'I told you to get back to work.'

'Havin' a drink.'

'I can see that,' she snapped. 'It's not what you're supposed to be doing.'

'George told me to shift some straw.'

'Well get back to it.'

Gavin put the basin down slowly, not moving his gaze from her. She moved to the door a little later to check on him. He was lifting straw lazily, a small bunch at a time, much of it dropping before it reached the wheelbarrow.

'Get on with it! Why don't you fasten it down? The wind'll have it out of the barrow before you get to the yards with it.'

'When I've loaded the barrer I will, with string. Look.' He held up a ball of twine.

The slowness of his movements goaded her. He seemed to be taunting her, but she did not have enough energy to persist and, feeling hungry, returned to the fireplace. She stirred the embers to warm what was left of the stew, until she heard a slight noise. Gavin had returned and was bending down by the table, looking for something. He stood up, as if he had not found it, and turned to leave without speaking to her.

'The jug of milk . . . have you seen it?' she yelled, noticing that his lips were white. He must have drunk the milk and had not wiped away the traces of scant cream that had risen to the surface. It was milk that she had set aside for Charles. However, Gavin had gone before she could accuse him. She followed him through the kitchen and outside to the door of the boys' room, where he stopped. He was strangely distracted, stooping as if he was still searching for something.

'What are you looking for?'

'Nothin'!'

'You couldn't look for less!'

Gavin continued to pace about.

'Are you losing your senses, boy?'

He did not reply but moved past her and began to trundle the wheelbarrow full of straw toward the yards. He had tied the string loosely, and left a trail of straw behind him. His strange head rocked backward and forward as he walked. She turned away in disgust.

9

Charles began to whimper again, so Mrs Pollard went back to nurse him in her bedroom. However, she soon felt uneasy, and putting Charles back in his cradle, she went to the door. There was no sign of Gavin.

She called out 'George', but there was no answer from the boys' room, so perhaps he had gone back to work. Feeling that something was amiss, she decided to see if he was there.

When she entered the room, George was on his bed, lying on his back. His coat was over his head, no doubt to keep off the flies. The poor boy must be exhausted.

'George,' she called.

As he did not stir, she called again twice, more loudly, 'George! George!' and shook him gently by the shoulder. But he still did not stir.

She pulled away the coat, saw that his pillow was soaked with blood, and thought that his nose must be bleeding. But there was a gash on it, and another on his temple. She put her right hand under his head, so that she could raise it, and felt a mash of bone and soft matter. When George breathed harshly and rapidly a few times, a rattling sound, she screamed and ran to the door.

Michael was the first to reach her. She could not speak, and pointed into the room behind her. Michael rushed in. He came out white-faced.

'What's happened, Mam? Mam . . . what's happened?'

'George! George . . . murdered! John Gavin must have . . .'

Michael moved away a few paces and vomited on the hot sand. A sour smell rose quickly from the mass of partly digested meat.

'Quickly, Michael! Run and fetch Mister Singleton, as quick as you can . . . Where's Tommy?'

'Still across the river.'

'I'll call him. Run . . . don't stop.'

Michael fled toward their neighbour's farm. Some minutes later, Tommy arrived, gasping for breath, as he had heard his mother's screams. He found her pacing in and out of the bedroom. He followed her into the room and she stooped to pick up an adze that was lying on the floor. She looked at its head, and was so numbed with horror she did not register at first that the bloody matter and hair adhering to the blade had come from her son.

'Mam! Mam!' Tommy's voice trailed away when he saw his brother. The sound of his voice broke through to his mother. She dropped the adze and stared at her bloodied hands.

'Tommy, George . . . George has been murdered! See the adze? Gavin!'

She asked Tommy to run for another neighbour, forgetting that this would leave her alone to confront Gavin. When Tommy had passed out of sight along the narrow track, she yelled for Gavin. He walked slowly toward her from the direction of the piggery. Suddenly afraid, she went back into the kitchen and grasped the board that Gavin had dropped near the dresser. When she went out again, Gavin was waiting at some distance from the house.

'Do you want me?' he asked. His apparent calmness disconcerted her.

'Where've you been?'

'To the river . . .' He gestured toward it. 'Near where them barrels are in it . . . fer a drink!'

'Why were you thirsty so soon? You drank Charlie's milk and a basin of water . . . I saw you had cream on your lips.'

Gavin wiped his lips self-consciously with the back of his hand.

'You murdered George!' she shouted.

'I didn't! Why do you say that?'

'Who else could've? There's no one else.'

'Mebbe some blacks! You wouldn't 'ear 'em comin'.'

'There were none today . . . none for some days. I saw you coming from the room.'

'P'raps George done 'imself.'

'You murdering villain! How could he . . . how could he hit himself on the back of his head?'

Gavin brushed past her and peered into the room, then came back to her. 'George won't say I done it,' he said.

'You didn't even let him breathe.'

Gavin called, 'George! George!'

Mrs Pollard tried to push him away from the bed.

Gavin shouted, 'Don't put that blood on me!'

She wiped her hands on her apron and then took it off and threw it away. She noticed that Gavin's shirt was wet. 'Have you been to wash the blood off your shirt?'

'No! I fell into the river when I was drinkin'.'

'Liar!' She tried to take hold of him, but he thrust out his hands to prevent her.

'Don't yer put that blood on me!' he yelled.

She put her apron around her hand, seized his shirt collar, and dragged the shirt from him. He stopped trying to resist. 'When Mister Singleton comes, I want him to see your shirt's wet.'

'I need another . . . I'm cold from fallin' in the river.' He followed her into the kitchen, pleading for another shirt.

She shut the bedroom door, to make sure that Charlie was safe, and picked up a cord that was lying on a chest. Gavin did not resist when she fastened it to his left wrist, but struggled when she attempted to tie the other. She was surprised to feel so strong; no weight now oppressed her limbs. He weakened and she managed to tie both wrists together. Thank goodness he was not a strong boy. She leant back against the wall, exhausted and trembling.

Gavin began to look about wildly and she was afraid that he might slip his bonds and escape, possibly attack her. She gathered her strength again and pushed him out the kitchen door and into George's room that had only one small window. She picked up the board that Gavin had brought, stood guard at the door while she waited for Singleton, and prayed that he would be at home when Michael got there.

Gavin managed to grab the board when she turned to see if anyone was coming. She should have tied his wrists behind him; terrified that Gavin would murder her, she struggled to wrench it back from him.

'I'll tell Mister Singleton you 'it me,' he said, moving toward her.

She backed out the door, and he dropped to his knees. 'Let me go, ma'am ... don't keep sayin' I murdered George. Let me go. I'll pray for George.'

'You pray? You devil!' She stepped back a pace, out of reach if he made a sudden lunge, and gripped the board more tightly. She was suddenly repulsed by the thought of striking that misshapen head, which might crack open like a melon.

Gavin kept pleading, over and over, 'I didn't murder 'im ... I'll pray ... I didn't murder 'im. Let me be ... I'll pray.'

She raised the board and shrieked, 'Stop! Stop! You didn't give George time to pray.'

'Knock me brains out,' he challenged her.

'I won't have your blood on my hands! Stop! Mister Singleton'll be here soon.'

He lurched to his feet suddenly and pushed his bound hands against her chest. His face was close to hers, his breath foul. 'I didn't do it ... I didn't ... I didn't!'

She was exhausted and the weight returned to her limbs. She made one last effort and heaved him away, catching him off balance, so he fell back and was winded. He lay there, catching his breath and began to gasp his litany of denial again.

'Thank God!' she said when she saw two red-jacketed soldiers approaching. She sank back on the chair, close to fainting. 'Thank God you're here, Corporal Alcock. Take this brute away from me.'

'Mister Singleton's away, ma'am, but should be back soon. We came straight away. We left your Michael to come with Mister Singleton.'

Corporal Alcock ordered the other soldier to bind Gavin more securely, to stand guard over him. The soldier jerked Gavin to his feet and pushed him in the direction of the carpenter's shop.

Mrs Pollard became aware of Charles's distressed crying. He had been neglected all this time. How long? Minutes? Hours? She went and picked up the baby before collapsing with him on the bed, where she lay back, clutching him and sobbing.

Singleton arrived late in the afternoon, with Michael. Mrs Pollard was asleep. The Corporal had lifted the baby from her and laid him in his cradle, for fear that he might fall from the bed. Singleton did not disturb Mrs Pollard, but went to take Gavin's deposition after visiting the nauseating scene of the murder.

10

Schoales had arranged to call on the Governor later in the day, to discuss his memorandum of proposals for changes to the juvenile immigration system. The Governor preferred to have regular verbal reports from his officials, leaving it to his Colonial Secretary, Peter Broun, to handle the paperwork.

Although it was early afternoon, the shadow of Mount Eliza had begun to relieve the heat in Schoales's office at the mill. He hoped to go again to his sister's house for the weekend. Only there could he feel at ease now, when so much pressed on him. He also planned to call at Mr Austin's on Monday, before returning to Perth, to check on Robinson, who had absented himself from work two or three times. He hoped that the boy would not relapse into his filthy habits again.

While waiting to walk to Government House, he filled in time practising the epistle, which his friend George King had asked him to read at St John's Church in Fremantle at one of the services for Lent. He needed to stem his rising doubt; if he lost his faith, what would there be in this colony to give him courage to persist? He was a little vain about his voice, and strove always to perfect it in singing or reading. He enjoyed the sonorities and rhythms of the King James Bible and of the Book of Common Prayer; when engaged by them he forgot doubt.

'We then, as workers together with him, beseech you also, that ye receive not the grace of God in vain: for he saith, I have heard thee in a time accepted, and the day of salvation – '

The sound of someone running up to his door interrupted him. He recognised Chief Constable Hester's voice calling for him, and opened the door. Hester was gasping for breath, 'Message just in from . . . Mister Singleton . . . at Dandalup . . . a terrible business . . . terrible.'

'What business?'

'Murder!'

'Murder?'

'Aye! Murder!' As Hester leant against the door, his shoulders drooped. Schoales gestured toward a chair and Hester sat down.

'Go on, Hester . . . Dandalup? I hope not the Pollards again.'

'Aye! The Pollards right enough. Their son George . . . murdered. Struck with an axe or an adze.'

Schoales gripped Hester's arm. 'Good God, Hester! Who could have done it . . . George? Why?'

'One of your boys, Mister Schoales, John Gavin! Mister Singleton has him in custody. He'll bring him up next week.'

Schoales sat down and rested his head in his hands for several moments and then glanced up at Hester. 'Dear God, is there no end to it?' A pang of pain in his chest made him catch his breath. When the spasm passed, he said, 'I thought the boy was going to be alright.'

Hester rested a hand on his shoulder. 'How were you to know this would happen, Mister Schoales? I'm sorry to bring such terrible news.'

'It was your duty, Hester. I'd planned to go up to Guildford this evening,' Schoales said. 'But I'd better wait here. As soon as you have any more information, come to me . . . at whatever hour.'

Schoales forgot his appointment with the Governor. He was summoned to a dressing-down on Monday morning. The Governor ended by pointing to Schoales's memorandum that lay on his desk. 'This is of little account now. I'll look at it after this appalling business has been dealt with.'

Richard Nash was at the mill when Schoales returned from his meeting with the Governor. Schoales had sent a message to his sister on Saturday morning to explain his absence.

'You must be devastated, John,' Nash said.

'Yes. I shouldn't have sent Gavin to the Pollards. They'll be distraught, so soon after Jane's death.'

'Don't blame yourself. The boy seemed to be alright when you went there.'

'I know . . . perhaps I missed something.'

'I'll handle the defence,' Nash said. 'As guardian, you can't. Have you heard any details yet?'

'No. I'm waiting to hear from Singleton.'

'Let me know when you have anything. I have to go, I'm due in court.' Nash gripped Schoales's shoulder. 'Don't sit here stewing while you wait.'

'I must wait until I hear more from Hester.'

'At least try and spend the weekend with us. I wouldn't be surprised if Lefroy turns up again. He's totally besotted with young Sophie, but he's always glad to see you. It might help if you talked things over with him.'

Schoales shook his head. 'I'll come when I can, but not until I have more information about this awful business.'

Soon after Nash left, some Parkhurst boys came to Schoales's office. Not one would speak up for Gavin.

'Who done it, sir?' one asked.

'Who do you think?'

'It was none off the *Simon Taylor*,' another boy responded quickly.

Schoales was amazed how the boys clung to those who voyaged with them – the *Simon Taylor* lads, the *Shepherd* lads – as if they had found new families.

'Was it George Clayton?'

'No.'

'Then it's gotta be John Gavin,' another boy said, without hesitation.

'Why Gavin?'

'He was the worst of us.'

Hester called late in the afternoon, with a message from Singleton; he planned to bring Gavin to Fremantle on Tuesday, as discreetly as possible, and would have him imprisoned in the Round House. Schoales knew that it would be impossible, given the macabre interest displayed by some people in the community, for Gavin and his escort to arrive unobserved. He had no wish to confront a crowd at the Round House, so deferred riding down to see Gavin until Wednesday morning. He hoped that he could then go to Elizabeth's for the weekend.

11

The sheriff greeted Schoales solemnly in his office. 'A nasty business, Mister Schoales. You'll want to see the prisoner.'

'Yes, Mister Stone. How does he seem?'

'Strangely calm ... shocked maybe. I'm not sure he's fully sensible of what he's accused. He doesn't seem sane to me. What a strange looking boy. I've had a chair put in his cell for you.'

This small courtesy touched Schoales, especially as the sheriff would not be pleased to have one accused of murder in his care.

'Has Mister Singleton stayed in town?' he asked. 'I need to talk to him. I need to know if there's any chance Gavin might be innocent ... or that there might be mitigating circumstances.'

'He didn't come. Two soldiers escorted the boy. Mister Singleton sent a message to say that he was much concerned about the Pollards. He wishes to give them some comfort as a neighbour, and to pursue inquiries.'

Sheriff Stone escorted Schoales to one of the tiny cells arrayed around the inside of the twelve-sided, roofless enclosure. When the sheriff unlocked the cell door and opened it, Schoales could see nothing in the gloom at first, his eyes still adapted to the glare from the limestone in the courtyard. The stench from the whalers' trypots on the beach at Bathers' Bay corrupted the air in the cell. Eventually he saw Gavin lying on the narrow bunk, with his face turned toward the wall. Schoales touched him on the shoulder and he rolled over and blinked at the light entering the open door. He smiled when he saw his guardian, which puzzled Schoales.

'Are you alright, John?'

'Hullo Mister Schoales . . . me wrists 'urt bad.' He held out both his arms. The ropes had left dark weals on the pale flesh of his thin wrists. The manacles, which had replaced the ropes, had chafed the weals, exposing raw flesh, which was now weeping. Schoales held both of Gavin's wrists and winced as he examined the lacerated flesh.

'This shouldn't have been done to you. I'll have some salve and bandages sent to you from the Depot.' He sat down and motioned Gavin to sit on the bed.

'Did you . . . did you murder George? They say you did.'

'I didn't. Missus Pollard lays it on me, but I didn't.'

'Are you sure? Can you swear to it?'

'George was me friend.'

The boy denied his guilt confidently, and Schoales could see no sign that Gavin was lying. He seemed calm and forthright. So far, he had only heard garbled accounts of the crime. He could not obtain copies of the depositions until Friday.

'You must be honest with me, John. You know that you can trust me as your guardian, your friend. Everything you say to me will be in confidence. I won't tell anyone else.'

'I didn't do it, sir!'

'I'll accept your word, for now. I can't say that things look good for you. I'll make sure you've a fair trial. Mister Nash'll defend you. I can't myself.'

Gavin nodded.

'Are you being treated well here?'

'Just me wrists!' He held out his arms again. In the dim light, the weeping weals were purplish.

'I'll go now and have salve and food sent to you. Are you sure there's nothing more?'

'Nothin'. I didn't do it. Yer gotta believe me.'

'I will, John!' Schoales wished he were more certain. 'I'll come again on Monday, after I've seen Mister Nash.'

Schoales returned to the sheriff's office.

The sheriff looked up and frowned. 'Well, Mister Schoales?'

'I see what you mean, Mister Stone. Until I spoke to him, I assumed, like everyone else it seems, that it was cut and dried, Gavin guilty. Now I've some doubt.' He paused, frowning. 'As you said, he's remarkably cool, detached and quite insensible of his awful plight, possibly unhinged.'

'It's a grim business,' the sheriff said. 'I'm not looking forward to it. I've been instructed to erect a gallows, in case ... I've never had to hang a boy before.'

Schoales was surprised that the erection of gallows had already been ordered. Had they made up their mind already?

'By the way, Mister Stone, I'll complain about the treatment of the lad. Did you see his wrists? Barbarous and unnecessary. I'll complain to his escort. I am sure Singleton would not have sanctioned this.'

The sheriff nodded. 'I've already done so,' he said.

Back at the Depot, a few boys gathered around Schoales and questioned him ghoulishly.

'Have yer seen Gavin, sir?'

'Yes. I've just come from him.'

'He'll 'ang fer it, won't 'e, sir?'

Schoales recalled the sheriff's grim face. 'If he's guilty . . . there has to be the trial first.'

'We all reckon 'e done it. He was about the worst o' the *Shepherd* lot.'

'I've not seen all the evidence yet, and Gavin denies it.'

'Well 'e would, wouldn't 'e?'

'Has no one of you a kind word for him? He's in need of comfort.'

Although one or two looked a little ashamed, no one spoke up for Gavin.

Next morning, when Schoales looked at his diary and found that the date was 29 February, he wondered if leap years were particularly ill favoured.

He had arranged to call early on Crown Solicitor Moore, to obtain copies of Singleton's depositions.

Moore was a large man, with an imposing presence; his heavy, dark eyebrows and dense mutton-chop whiskers framed strong, but sensitive features. He was well known for relishing his food and drink, and delighting in all social gatherings. His rollicking baritone had sometimes supported Schoales in a ballad.

He rifled through a sheaf of papers, to check that they were complete, before handing them to Schoales, then mopped his bald dome with a large handkerchief, the morning being warm and humid.

'Who'll defend? I don't suppose you will, as Gavin's one of your wards.'

'Richard ... Richard Nash, my brother-in-law.'

'Of course! It will be an interesting case but, from what I've heard, not much to mount in defence. But Richard's a doughty defender. It will be Irish against Irish again. That should keep us on our mettle.' He glanced at Schoales and, noticing his expression, added, 'I'm sorry. This must be a blow for you, as your boys seem to be going well in general. Don't take it too hard, personally.'

'I've spoken to Gavin, and I now feel a little doubt about his guilt. He denied it confidently ... perhaps I'm reading too much into that. I need to read these.' He tapped the sheaf of papers that he held. 'I'll also want to speak to Singleton, and I intend to ask Hester to make some inquiries.'

'By the way, Schoales, I've heard some talk that Gavin's a Roman, and you're denying him a fellow-Roman's comfort. What's going on? Some of the Romans are saying that the Pollards persecuted Gavin because he was one of them.'

'I saw no sign of it when I visited the family, although I believe they've Orange tendencies. Gavin's listed as a Catholic in the records,' Schoales said. 'But I doubt if he's been to a church in many a year. He went to Parkhurst when he was only twelve, although I believe there was a Catholic chaplain there. In the months he was at the Depot, he showed no signs of religion. Anyhow, I don't think the boy's sane.' He put the copies of the depositions in his satchel. 'I suppose that we shouldn't be discussing this, since you'll be prosecuting.'

'It's a grim matter, but there may be some important

points of law in this ... precedents,' Moore said. 'This is the first murder trial for a white man of another white man ... damn it, boys. That's worse in a way.' He punched his right fist against the palm of his left hand. 'We have to see the law well founded here. Don't forget to tell Richard that I'm looking forward to our contest.'

Schoales took the depositions to his office and read them attentively, underscoring some words and passages, and annotating the margins. Mrs Pollard's evidence was damning but uncorroborated. She was the only material witness. He sensed her riven heart under the strange, detached quality of her account. That tone might be due to Singleton's rendering, although he had no doubt of the magistrate's commitment to recording the facts truly. No one else had witnessed the murder, and there were some inconsistencies in her and the other depositions. He thanked God that Richard would have the job of questioning her, knowing that he could not himself. He would be able to discuss it with him during the weekend.

12

On Saturday, Schoales rode out early to see Richard, anxious to discuss the depositions with him. His horse sensed that he was not at ease, and cantered nervously. Schoales patted its neck. 'Gently Samson, be thankful that you're out of human affairs.'

He began to feel more at ease as he reached the farmlands on the way to his sister's house. In the colony, the month of March was officially the first of autumn, although some days could be hot and oppressive. This morning, however, was cool, and high cirrus clouds signalled that summer was ending and the first autumn rains might come soon. That season, here, was more like spring at home; the early rains caused weeds and crops to germinate while the weather was still warm, more like the burgeoning at home after the long chill of winter.

Elizabeth waited anxiously for her brother and hurried to the door when she saw that his face was pinched, and the ride from Perth had restored only a little colour to his cheeks. When he and Richard retreated to the parlour, his walk had lost its spring. She knew that Richard had no doubt of Gavin's guilt, and hoped that John was not expecting otherwise.

Before he read the depositions, Nash asked Schoales what he thought.

'I've spoken to Gavin. He seems strangely calm, and

protests his innocence ... did so repeatedly when I questioned him. The depositions are fairly damning, but there are
some inconsistencies. I've marked them, as you'll see. No one
witnessed the murder.'

'Let me study these awhile. Talk to Elizabeth while I'm
doing so.'

Elizabeth offered him tea and then began recounting
local gossip to divert him.

'Don't be surprised if Gerald appears during the weekend,'
she said. 'I heard that the Roes are expecting him again.'

'Richard says he's besotted with that girl.'

'One or two others are as well, I hear,' Elizabeth said.
'That must be why Gerald rides down from York whenever
he can.'

Schoales smiled wanly. 'I told him that I won't be one of
his rivals. I'm a good ten years older than he is ... much too
old for Sophie.'

Elizabeth reached across the table to grasp his arm. 'You
should find more time to meet other families,' she said.

'I just don't have time. I thought I might be getting on top
of things ... then this business – '

Elizabeth frowned. 'Don't take it so much to heart, John.
No one can blame you. Those boys aren't angels ... some are
sure to offend again.'

'I know, but most of their offences are minor ...' He drew
a deep breath and sighed. 'Some people are saying I've not
been strict enough, and do lay some blame on me.'

'Nonsense! Ignorant gossip! Those who know better won't
hold it against you.'

'Even the papists are at it now. They say the lad's one of them –'

'That's spiteful, John,' she said.

Richard called from the parlour, 'Are you going to gossip all day with Elizabeth, John? I'm ready to talk about this business.'

Schoales smiled at Elizabeth and shrugged his shoulders as he went to join Richard.

Richard stood up when Schoales joined him, and said, 'Well, John, I think I can make out a defence, but there's not a lot to go on. I'll have to work on the jury. Their sympathy will be with the Pollards, of course.' He gestured to the book-case. 'I must read *Oliver Twist* again. Then I could lay it on like Dickens and waken some sympathy. You know the sort of thing, a poor child led into crime despite himself. Unfortunately, there's no one I can name as his Fagin. You certainly don't qualify, even if you're in charge of these boys ... by the way, is there anything in his record about previous violence?'

'Nothing. As I was saying to Moore, most of the boys have only been involved in thieving ... Moore's looking forward to locking you in combat.'

Elizabeth joined them, and protested. 'It's not a game.'

'More like theatre,' Richard said. 'We've only two chances. Firstly, to convince the jury that the evidence is not conclusive, mostly circumstantial. That won't be easy. Justice Mackie's determined to discourage lawlessness, especially as some people are beginning to advocate transporting adult convicts here.'

'The second thing?' Schoales asked.

'If the worst comes to the worst, an appeal for clemency. There's Gavin's age, and the question of his sanity. Then, what was that about his misshapen head?'

'I wondered if it might be hydrocephaly, but I doubt if anyone in the colony could verify it,' Schoales said. 'However, I can't see Hutt being clement, after that reproof he got from Lord Russell for granting a reprieve for one of those natives sentenced for murder.'

'But we need to be ready,' Nash said. 'I'll prepare an appeal for you to have ready in case. When's the trial?'

'A month from now ... first week in April, Wednesday the third.'

Richard consulted a pocket almanac. 'Mother of God! That's the Wednesday before Easter. But that might work to our advantage; they might not want to hang the poor wretch at Easter time.'

'Hutt'll have a chance to play Pilate,' Schoales said bitterly.

'John! That's blasphemous!' Elizabeth exclaimed.

'I'm sorry, Elizabeth. I only meant that he might wash his hands of any appeal to mercy.' He turned to Nash. 'I could try to have it set for a later date.'

Gerald Lefroy arrived during the afternoon. Elizabeth invited him to stay for supper; he might divert her brother, who had been moody and unnaturally quiet since lunch. She asked him not to talk about the nasty business of the murder, or Sophie either, wondering again if John would ever find a loving companion to help him set aside his worries. She felt blessed by her marriage to Richard.

Schoales said little during the meal, despite all efforts to engage him. When the meal finished, Elizabeth was pleased when Lefroy asked her brother to walk him part of the way back to Sandalford.

'You look as if you need exercise, John,' Lefroy said.

Schoales nodded. 'A walk might help me to sleep,' he said. 'I'm desperately tired, and I should go back to Perth tomorrow morning. I must call on Austin first, as he's nearby. I need to see how that lad Robinson ... the one I've told you about ... has settled in.'

'Don't go so soon,' Elizabeth said. 'You need a longer break.'

Schoales stood up. 'I need to be on hand, in case anything develops. Come on then, Gerald,' he said. Turning to his sister, he added, 'Don't wait up for me.'

Elizabeth doubted if she would be able to go to sleep until she knew that he had returned.

The moon was nearly full, so Schoales and Lefroy were able to follow the track without a lantern. Lefroy led his horse by its halter. Schoales rested his hand on the horse's shoulder, comforted by the warmth and the movement of its muscles.

'It's cold, tonight,' Schoales said, buttoning up his cloak.

'A mite cool, perhaps,' Lefroy said. 'Let's walk more briskly.'

After they had walked a little way, Schoales asked, 'How's Sophie?'

'To tell you the truth, John, I don't think things are going so well now. It's difficult when I'm a long day's ride away ...

such a young girl can be diverted easily. Have you thought any more about what you'll do?'

'I've been considering resigning my post and taking on more law work. The stipend's not big enough, and I sometimes have to wait months to have my travel costs refunded, so I haven't cleared my debts yet … but I can't resign until I've seen this business through … the trial … and – ' he choked. 'I can't bear to think what might happen if the wretch is found guilty.' Schoales stopped. 'I'm too tired to go further,' he said. 'When this is all over, I hope I can take a break … maybe go with you when you go looking for land again.'

Lefroy laid his hand on his friend's shoulder. 'I'll hold you to that,' he said.

Lefroy mounted. Schoales stood until his friend passed out of sight at a bend in the track. He turned to walk back, but paused again to listen to the noises of the night. There was a chuckling sound from the river, probably a wood duck. Then an owl called somewhere nearby, softer than that of the common barn owl at home, just two syllables, 'boo-book'. But he could not hear the 'k' at the end of the call, so it sounded more like the cuckoo at home. When he had first heard it, he thought it was another example of the topsy-turvy nature of this country, that cuckoos should sing at night. Tonight the call sounded mournful and feeling alienated, he yearned shelter. He began to walk more quickly, but checked his pace when he stumbled on a tree root.

In the morning, as she watched her brother ride away, Elizabeth embraced her husband and said, 'I fear for John; he's too much on his own.'

Austin's farm was only half an hour's ride from the Nash's. Austin was examining his vines close to the track, and walked toward Schoales as he dismounted.

'It's good of you to call,' Austin said, 'especially at a time like this . . . a sad business.'

'I was at my sister's, so it was convenient. I want to check on Robinson. Has he been disobedient again?'

'No, he seems to have settled. The last time, I think he was provoked by another of your lads who spoke to him as he passed on his way to a new master.'

'That was probably Henry Walls on his way to Parker's place at York. Mister Jecks was to give him a lift from here. But they all seem to delight in taunting Robinson. Did Henry seem alright?'

'Yes, why?'

'He's had trouble with his eyes and some infection on his legs. I made sure he had eye water and dressings before he left the Depot . . . I have to keep an eye on the lads' health as well as their behaviour.'

'Overseeing just one of your lads is enough for me,' Austin said. 'I don't know how you manage so many.'

'It sounds as if you've had more trouble with Robinson. I'll speak to him, where is he?'

'He's in the vineyard.'

They found Robinson hoeing some weeds between the

vines. The boy looked sturdier and had a good colour from working in the open.

'Good morning, Edward. I'm glad to hear that you've not run off again. Here ...' Schoales handed the boy a small book. 'Something for you to read.'

The boy smiled as he took the book. He seemed so pleasant when he was not afflicted by his temporary insanities. Perhaps he would not relapse again, or not so often.

Schoales patted Robinson on the shoulder. 'Ned, you're lucky to have a kindly master like Mister Austin. You must not run away from him again. Do you promise?'

Robinson did not speak, but nodded.

Austin walked with Schoales as he returned to his horse. When Schoales mounted he reached up to shake his hand. Schoales took comfort from the strength of his grip.

'Let me know immediately, if you have any more trouble with him,' he said as he prepared to leave.

'I'll make sure he works most of the time at the far end of the vineyard, away from the track ... out of the way of any other lads who might be passing.'

'That's kind of you. I hope he responds.'

13

On Monday morning, Schoales sent for Chief Constable Hester, who soon arrived, mopping his forehead with his handkerchief. The morning was warm and muggy, and he had trotted part of the way.

'Sit down, Hester. I appreciate you coming so promptly. I'd like you to conduct further inquiries at Dandalup,' Schoales said.

Hester took out his notebook.

'Don't bother to take notes. I've written instructions for you. There are some inconsistencies in the depositions taken by Singleton. See if you can find out more about how Gavin got on with the Pollard family, George particularly –' Schoales broke off to look at his notes. Hester sat forward in his chair, as Schoales was speaking more softly. 'There's some talk that the two boys quarrelled, but I had the impression, when I was last there, that he and George were good friends. The natives, too. Gavin blames natives for the murder in his deposition. Check if there were any in the district at the time of the murder ... I believe there are fewer near the settled areas now ... and if there'd been any trouble between them and the settlers lately, the Pollards particularly.'

Hester sat back. 'I'll do my best. However –' he frowned. 'As you say, some of the evidence may've been destroyed. At least there's been no rain there since ... since the day of the murder ... so some signs may still be there.'

'Good man. Do what you can. Mister Nash will be defending the boy, and he says we need more hard evidence.'

'For the defence?'

'Evidence, Hester, facts – however they fall. Gavin has to be presumed innocent for now.'

'Surely. Is there anything else I should look into?'

'Get hold of a native tracker, if you can, and check if Gavin went to the river as he claimed, though it may now be too late to find any signs that he fell in. He says he fell in at a spot to the left of the house, when you're facing the river, about fifty yards from the barn – ' Short of breath, he recalled the peaceful scene of the farm in the evening light. 'These inquiries are to be conducted confidentially. I have sealed your instructions. Don't open them until you get to the Dandalup. Exercise discretion and be as quick as you can. There's little time, as the trial is four weeks from now, the third of April. Let me know by mail if you find anything of consequence.'

As soon as Hester left, taking the copies of the depositions with him, Schoales gathered his papers and set out for the livery stable. When he arrived, he was told that Samson was at the farrier to be reshod.

'Damn it!' Schoales said. 'I thought I could rely on you.'

He felt ill at ease on an unfamiliar mount as he set out for Fremantle to see Gavin again.

As he approached Arthur's Head, Schoales was disturbed to see several workmen clearing ground to the right of the stairs, where the gallows were to be erected. The men touched their

hats and greeted him cheerfully, as if they were untroubled by
the task they had been given.

When Schoales entered the cell, Gavin was lying on his
bunk, and he was surprised to see him so calm.

'Good morning, John,' Schoales said. 'How are you?'

'Orright! Me wrists're better,' He held out his arms. The
weals on his wrists had healed.

'That's good. Now, I'm going to read what you and Missus
Pollard said to Mister Singleton.' He held up the sheaf of
papers. 'Listen carefully.'

He read Gavin's own testimony first. When he had
finished, he asked, 'Are you sure that that is what you said to
Mister Singleton?'

'Yes! Near so! I told 'im, as it says on the paper, that I
didn't do it. I told 'im that Missus Pollard laid it on me. I told
'im, as it says there, about 'er pushing me with 'er bloody
hands … I told 'im all that.'

'Alright! Now I'll read Missus Pollard's depos … what she
said to Mister Singleton. Were you there when he talked
to her?'

'No! They shut me up in the carpen'er's shop.'

Schoales read more of Mrs Pollard's statement.

Gavin became agitated and spoke as soon as Schoales
finished. 'She's still layin' it on me. I didn't do it.'

In the dim light, Gavin's pale skin glowed eerily. He had
lost weight and grown pale from confinement. His ungainly
head rocked rapidly from side to side. Schoales was not
sure what he could read in the lad's face, his almost expres-
sionless eyes.

'John, don't turn your head away when I ask a question,' Schoales said. 'Look at me straight. Did you murder George?'

'Are you layin' it on me too?' Gavin's face fired up with anger.

'No, but that's the sort of question you'll be asked at your trial. Mister Nash will need to be sure of your answers.'

'I didn't do it.' The answer had begun to sound like an obsessional refrain. The lad glared at Schoales, mistrusting him now. His eyelids fluttered as if the light irritated his eyes like grits.

Schoales rose from the chair, his legs stiff from sitting in the confined space.

'I'll do all I can for you, John,' he said, but was troubled that he might not be able to do enough, particularly as he had seen the preparations for the erection of the gallows.

He stood for a few moments in the doorway of the cell, until he was sure that his voice would be steady, before he spoke. 'I'll go back to Perth now. If you need to talk to me, ask Mister Stone to send me a message.'

He backed out of the cell and slammed the door. The twelve-sided prison focussed the glare and heat, and he rested awhile on the low parapet of the well in its centre, trying to overcome the nausea and the sense of menace that had come upon him suddenly in the foetid cell.

During the troubled week, Schoales found the late burst of heat even more oppressive, and slept badly. He welcomed a visit by Nash, who called on him at the mill early on Friday.

He had come to find out if anything had been elicited from Gavin about the depositions.

'One thing might be useful, Richard.'

Nash was doodling in the dust on top of a cupboard he was leaning on. 'Doesn't anyone ever dust in here?'

'Gavin seems emphatic that the blood on his shirt came from Missus Pollard's hand when she pushed him, and I've sent Hester to enquire into some things that seem inconsistent in the depositions.'

'Have you heard anything from him?'

'Nothing yet. I expect him any day.'

'We shouldn't count on much, but anything might help. We've little enough for the defence case and we've only a little over two weeks before the trial. Let's talk more about it this evening. Elizabeth is anxious to see you.'

'And I to see her of course. I can leave soon, when I've tidied up a few things.'

There was a knock at the door. Schoales opened it, to a warder from the Round House.

'What's happened?' Schoales asked.

'The sheriff asked me to tell you that Gavin wishes to see you most particularly.'

'Dammit!' Schoales said. 'I'm sorry, I don't mean you.' He handed the warder some coins. 'Thank you for delivering the message. Get yourself some refreshment before you go back to Fremantle.'

Schoales turned to Nash. 'I hope the boy's really got something to say.'

'You don't have to go at once. Why not wait until after

the weekend?' Nash asked. 'Elizabeth will be disappointed . . . so will I.'

'I wish I could, but if Gavin stews on it for another two days he might not be ready to talk. Perhaps he wants to confess.'

'It'd be better if he did,' Nash said. 'It would save Missus Pollard an ordeal.'

'You sound as if you've given up on him,' Schoales said.

'Not entirely. But it seems that no one will come out unscathed by this.'

'I'll certainly be glad when it's all over, one way or another,' Schoales said.

Schoales was glad to find that Samson was available at the livery stable. He was a little more at ease during his ride to Fremantle, although he felt despondent when he arrived at the Round House. Gavin was asleep when he was ushered into the cell. He shook the boy to wake him.

Gavin shielded his eyes from the light. 'Mister Schoales!'

'You sent for me, John. Have you something to tell me?'

'I didn't kill George . . . not what Missus Pollard keeps layin' on me.'

'For God's sake, boy! So you've told me repeatedly.' He could not hide his impatience, 'I came down especially . . . I thought you might have something else to tell me.'

'I wasn't sure you believed me.'

'I'm doing my best to do so. I keep telling you.'

'I didn't.'

'I must go, John. There seems no point in my staying.

I will only come again if I have something to tell you, or if you really have something else to tell me.' He could no longer bear to be in the cell, and decided that he would not come again, unless convinced it was necessary.

Schoales returned to Perth, hoping to go on to Elizabeth's house later. However, there was a message left under the door of his office to say that Hester had advised that he would be back in Perth on Sunday, the following day, and would call on Schoales as soon as he arrived.

Hester reported that he had not been able to find any substantial evidence to counter or verify the depositions gathered by Singleton, although he was certain that no natives had been involved.

'I think that all I managed to do,' he said, 'was to give that poor family more pain by my inquiries.'

Schoales, sensing the distressed tone of Hester's remark, wondered if there would ever be an end of pain for anyone touched by the tragedy.

On Monday, he called at Nash's Perth office to tell him of Hester's report on his inquiries.

'I wasn't hopeful that he'd find anything significant,' Nash said. 'I hadn't counted on him doing so.'

'Any word about the date of the trial?' Schoales asked.

'I've just had word that Mackie won't change the date,' Nash said.

'We have only two weeks. My God! I'll be glad when it's all over,' Schoales said. 'I'm finding it hard to settle to anything.'

'Why not take some time off?'

'What would I do?'

'Didn't you say something about going with Gerald on one of his exploration trips?'

'He won't go again until after the rains. The country'll be too dry now to judge its quality.'

'Come to us whenever you need to,' Nash said.

'Thank you, of course. I'd better go back to my office now. I've not been through my mail.'

Schoales deliberately chose a longer route to walk back, partly for exercise, and partly to fill in time. When he returned to his office, he found among his mail, letters from several masters, who were having minor problems with boys assigned to them. He decided that he would travel extensively over the following three weeks, to deal with these issues and to check on other boys, especially those of whom he had not had reports for some time. It would fill in most of the time until the trial, and would provide some distraction from the sense of dread that obsessed him.

He set out two days later, heading south to start with, where it would be cooler, and deliberately travelled more slowly than usual. Most of the boys that he visited had settled in well with their masters; the problems of the others were settled amicably. However, he still frequently had troubled nights.

14

William Mackie, Chairman of the Quarter Sessions, antici-
pating that many would attend the trial, had asked for extra
chairs to be placed in the small Courthouse. The trial was due
to begin at half past ten. Some people, including Nash and
Schoales, waited outside for the arrival of the prisoner.
Besides the constables on duty, a detachment of soldiers
waited nearby.

Nash pointed to the soldiers. 'Mackie asked for them,' he
said, 'but I don't think he expects trouble. It's more for show.
He told me once that he thought we did things meanly here;
there was more pomp and ceremony in India.'

Someone cried out, 'Here they come!'

The initial buzz of excitement faded quickly and silence
prevailed as Gavin was led past by two constables; a thin,
pale boy with a grotesque head, which seemed too heavy for
the boy's thin neck. Manacles weighed down his thin arms – it
was a wonder they were not wrenched from their sockets – and
they clanked as he was led to the side entrance of the
Courthouse. Some of the people moved away, as if they had
lost the desire to witness.

Nash and Schoales moved inside, and Gavin looked toward
them as they took their seats. Schoales raised his hand in
acknowledgement. Mackie entered shortly afterward, and
called for silence – a formality, because those within the court
had fallen silent when the prisoner entered.

Mackie adjusted his wig and addressed the court. 'My legal colleagues, gentlemen of the jury, fellow citizens, this is a solemn occasion – the most solemn that it has been my lot to preside over since I came here. This is the first trial in the colony of an Englishman – an English boy – for murder . . .' A moment passed before he added, 'of another English boy.'

Schoales heard several in the gallery gasp; one woman sitting close behind him sobbed briefly.

'I call the first witness, Missus Pollard,' Mackie said.

Mrs Pollard began to stand, but slumped back on her chair. Her husband took her arm and helped her to rise and walk the short distance to the witness stand. There was a sympathetic murmur from the gallery. The changes in her appearance shocked Schoales. Her hair was noticeably greyer and her face engraved with new lines. She also appeared to have lost weight.

Moore, a skilled advocate, modulated his voice like an actor, and gestured like the conductor of an orchestra as he began to question her.

Mrs Pollard stood erect, although her shoulders were bowed, and she spoke in a calm, but distracted, voice. Its tone was uncannily the same as in Singleton's record of her deposition. She appeared to function mechanically, and Schoales felt guilty that he had recently been obsessed by his own concern for the fate of his ward, to the exclusion of everything else. He felt as if he had been travelling in a dark tunnel and could see no opening ahead.

'I remember the day well,' she began. 'Ash Wednesday it was, at about the middle of the day . . . John Gavin – '

'Please refer to him as the accused or as the prisoner,' Mackie said.

She recounted the events of the terrible day, much as in her deposition. She spoke of calling Gavin and her boys to lunch, and how she had felt so heavy. 'It was so soon after my daughter's death . . .' For a moment, it seemed that her strange calm might desert her, but she carried on after only a brief pause, to describe what happened next.

Some jurors leant forward, deeply engaged by what she said, and there was total silence in the court until she resumed.

Moore's voice – that rich baritone, so often raised in song – was soft when he resumed questioning, as if he wished to entice answers gently. His questions focussed on the strongest points of the evidence for the prosecution; they were also points that would most arouse the jurors' sympathy for Mrs Pollard.

'In your deposition, you say the prisoner brought a piece of board to you when you were asleep,' he said. 'Did you think he would strike you, and, if so, why?'

'No, although I *was* alarmed. He should have been helping George with fencing. I'd been sharp with him often, for impudence or disobedience. I was very angry then, as well . . . about the jug of milk I was keeping for Charlie, my baby son. We'd little enough as the cows were dry. He was . . . he's very poorly.' She was now close to breaking down.

Schoales sensed a wave of sympathy for Mrs Pollard welling up in the court, and the increasing tension as, still in monotone, she approached the critical point of her testimony. He looked at Gavin, whose head was turned toward a window at the back of the courtroom, as though watching a passing cloud or bird.

Moore stroked his whiskers, as if he was pondering deeply, and asked Mrs Pollard what happened then.

'Something didn't seem right, so I went to the boys' room. George was lying on his bed. I called him two or three times, but he didn't answer ... he didn't move. Poor boy, I thought, he must be exhausted. He always works hard, even harder when my husband's away.'

Schoales glanced at John Pollard, who was sitting between his sons Michael and Tommy. How must he feel to have been absent that day?

'I walked up to his bed, and shook him by the shoulders. The coat – he had it over his head to stop the flies, I thought – slipped off him. There was blood on the pillow ...'

There were murmurs of horror from the body of the court, and some people strained on the edge of their seats. Gavin turned to look at the people, as if he was surprised by the commotion. Schoales was sure that the boy had lost his reason.

'There was a gore of blood ... there were cuts on his face ... but, when I put my hand under the back of his head ...' She paused to wipe her hand vigorously against her dress. 'It sank into a mash of bone and –'

There were horrified gasps and an outbreak of talk. Mackie called for silence. When order had been restored, Moore, bending slightly from the waist as if in deference to Mrs Pollard, asked gently, so gently that several members of the jury held their hands to their ears to catch the words, 'Can you go on, Missus Pollard?'

'Yes . . . yes, I can!'

Nash nudged his brother-in-law. 'He has the jury where he wants them. I'll have to undo all that, somehow.'

Mrs Pollard resumed, describing how she had accosted Gavin and despatched her sons for help. Moore interrupted more frequently with questions, to fix the jury's attention on each horrible detail.

'I want to go back to something. You state that, when you were lying down, your heard your son singing, or you thought you did.'

'Yes, I thought it was George, but I'd been asleep and I might've dreamt it. That hymn was in a book he'd borrowed. Afterward, I looked in the book for the words but couldn't find them at first . . . as the pages were stuck together with blood.'

Mackie again called the court to order.

Moore finished with questions about the bloodstains on Gavin's shirt. Mrs Pollard admitted that she had pushed Gavin when her hands were bloodied.

Schoales whispered to Nash, 'That might be one in our favour.'

Moore bowed slightly and said, 'Thank you, Missus Pollard. I'll spare you any more questions.'

Schoales thought that was cunning; Moore was suggesting that she had been questioned enough, but Nash would have to question her now and, as the antagonist, would find it hard to engage the sympathy of the jury.

Nash gained time by perusing his notes, allowing the jury

to be distracted. He began with relatively innocuous questions, speaking gently. Schoales had seen Nash use this tactic before; he was trying to cloud the jury's memory of some key points of Mrs Pollard's evidence, and preparing to deal with the weaker points of the prosecution. He frequently nodded, as he always did when speaking in court. Schoales wondered if Nash knew that he had a nickname, 'Noddy'.

He asked questions about George and Gavin getting on well together.

'Yes. I remember one day, when I was having words with the prisoner, George told him to come away and not to stand being blowed up by me like that.'

Nash raised his eyebrows as he glanced at the jury, but Schoales was not sure if this was a good line to pursue. The jury might think that Gavin would not kill a friend, but they might harden against him if they thought that he had.

Nash asked whether she had heard any sounds of a struggle from the boys' bedroom.

She shook her head.

Nash asked, 'Was your son bigger or smaller than the accused?'

'Bigger. Taller and stronger. He's ... he was a good, strong boy.'

Mrs Pollard began to sway, and gripped the rail. Her face was bloodless.

Nash turned to Mackie. 'Your Honour, I think the witness isn't well. I will spare her any further questions. Thank you, Missus Pollard.' He looked at the jury and thought they might be a shade less hostile to the defence.

Mackie asked Mrs Pollard if she would like to stand down.

'I'd rather go on ... be done with it sooner.'

Mackie instructed that a chair be brought to the stand, and told her she could sit. Nash gave her time to become composed, and then asked if the bloodstains on Gavin's shirt may have been from a slaughtered beast, not her own hands.

'Possibly, but it was some time since we'd slaughtered a beast.'

'Thank you, Missus Pollard,' he said. 'I'm sorry you've had such an ordeal. I've only one more question. When Mister Singleton arrived and questioned you, was the prisoner present?'

'No, he'd been taken away by then.'

Nash thanked her and said he had no more questions. Mrs Pollard walked slowly and unsteadily to sit with her husband and her sons. Her husband put his arm around her and she dropped her head on his shoulder.

Mackie said, 'It is midday. I will close proceedings for an hour.'

The courthouse became noisy as those in the gallery stood and began to talk animatedly as they moved towards the door. Mrs Pollard remained seated until the court was empty. Her husband then led her and his sons to an adjoining room.

15

During the break, Schoales and Nash walked to Henry Strickland's hotel in Saint George's Terrace, handy to the Courthouse. Nash ordered a pork pie and a pint of ale and ate heartily, but Schoales only toyed with a beef sandwich. He was thirsty though, and his throat was dry, probably due to the tension he had felt during the morning sitting, so he also drank a pint of ale.

'What're your impressions, Richard?' Schoales asked.

'I've not changed my opinion. I still think the boy's guilty, but I think that the evidence isn't enough to find him so. Moore has the jury on his side, although there are one or two things that I may be able to do to cause them to think hard before they decide ... Perhaps it's good that they heard Missus Pollard first. The other witnesses may not evoke their sympathies so strongly.'

Schoales nodded.

Nash noticed that he was pale. 'You should take leave after this is over, John.'

'I will, but I've no idea what I'll do after that. My mind isn't clear at all.'

'Will your resign your post?'

'I'd thought I would, but I'm not sure now. It would seem that I was running away from everything.'

'No one would think that, John,' Nash said.

'My own conscience might be troubled, though.'

'Sometimes your conscience is too nice,' Nash said. He glanced at his watch. 'We must go back. This will be the critical session for me.'

When the court reopened, Singleton was called, and he confirmed that Mrs Pollard's account was substantially the same as the deposition he had taken. Moore asked what he found when he went to the Pollards' farm.

'I went into the room, a lean-to at the side of the house,' he said, 'to examine the body of the deceased. It was lying on a bed ... on its back. There was a gash across the cheekbone and nose, and one on the temple. The back of the head was cleft in pieces, and the wounds ran into each other ... and two fingers had been severed.' The dispassionate tone of his voice made his graphic account even more repulsive.

Schoales, sensing the revulsion of the people in the court, looked at Gavin, who had not moved since he last looked at him. He seemed frozen, as though he still had not heard anything, or did not understand if he had.

When Moore had finished, Nash muttered to Schoales, 'I think I have an opening.'

He rose and asked, 'Mister Singleton, you described the wounds to the face of the victim, in addition to the gashes on the skull. You also said a couple of fingers were severed. They must have been heavy blows.'

Singleton nodded. 'The head of the adze was heavy ... a normal swing of it would be sufficient.'

'Did you believe that there was a struggle, that the victim attempted to ward off blows? He was, I understand, a strong boy ... stronger than the accused.' He gestured toward Gavin.

'Yes, it's possible that there was a struggle, but he may have slept with his hand across his face.'

The acting Colonial Surgeon, Joseph Harris, was called next. Moore had only one statement. 'Surely the infliction of such horrendous wounds would have caused considerable noise.'

'Some noise, but most likely thuds rather than sharp sounds. If there was a struggle there might have been other noises, such as shouting or knocking sounds.'

Schoales was shocked by the graphic description, spoken unemotionally.

Nash asked Harris, 'Were the wounds consistent with the exhibited adze, and do you believe that the accused was strong enough to inflict those wounds?'

'I am certain on both of those points. However, I was surprised that Missus Pollard said that the deceased had breathed when she tried to move him. I believe that the wounds would have caused death almost immediately ... It might have been a post-mortem spasm of some kind.'

Nash said, 'No more questions.' He turned to face Mackie and began a detailed argument about matters of law. 'We all hope,' he said, 'that there will never be another trial here for murder, but human beings are not perfect and another such case is probable in the future and this case will be a precedent. I remind the jury of the danger of relying on circumstantial evidence. There've been cases in England where the accused were found guilty and suffered the extreme penalty, but re-examination of cases sometimes led to posthumous pardon.'

He paused. Schoales knew that what Nash would now say might be a critical turning point in the trial.

Nash continued, 'I'll return to that argument when I examine the prosecution case in detail. However, there's another matter, a point of law, which should be dealt with first. I refer to the evidence that the committing magistrate took Missus Pollard's deposition when the accused was not present. At home, statute now requires the accused to be present at all depositions. In fact, Your Honour, in the eye of the law, the prisoner should not be considered on trial at all. The case should be dismissed.'

Uproar broke out. The jurymen talked among themselves. Mackie rapped violently with his gavel and the noise died down. He announced an adjournment while the bench considered the defending counsel's learned argument.

When Mackie returned, he announced that the court was decidedly of the opinion that the learned counsel's objection was not valid, since all the witnesses were present and had given evidence again in the presence of the prisoner.

Nash snorted and turned to Schoales. 'Prepare to ask the Governor for clemency, John.'

Mackie asked Nash if he wished to continue his address to the jury.

'Thank you, yes Your Honour. The entire prosecution case depends upon uncorroborated evidence of one material witness. I do not reflect in any way on the good character, in every respect, of that witness. I only argue that there are inconsistencies in the witness's testimony, and suggest, with the deepest sympathy, that her comprehension of the events of the day, and her memory of them, must have been affected deeply by all her grievous sufferings. We have also heard of her antipathy to the prisoner and of her problems with him ... understandable in the circumstance.'

Nash paused again, glanced at his notes, and continued, 'No motive for the crime had been suggested and the prisoner continues to deny guilt resolutely, and made no attempt to flee from the scene, although he must have had the opportunity to do so.'

The court was now hushed. Nash lowered his voice to make his listeners strain to hear him and to ensure that they would remain hushed. 'There are points of evidence that are, to say the least, perplexing. The witness heard, or thought she heard the deceased singing through the partition, but heard nothing else. Her son breathed his last in her presence, so the wounds must have been inflicted only minutes before, yet Missus Pollard heard no other voice, and no sounds of a struggle or blows.'

He broke off, removed his spectacles – he did not want any light reflected from the lenses to shield his eyes from the jury – and placed his notes on the desk before him. When he resumed, he allowed his gaze to rest on each member of the jury in turn, challenging him. 'Gentlemen. A possibility is never a certainty. If you have any doubts, you cannot find the prisoner guilty.'

He held the jury in suspense again for a minute or two. 'Gentlemen, you have a double charge today. You have to determine your verdict in this tragic case. You also have to help to establish British justice here in the colony on a sound base. Remember the awful consequences that will flow from a guilty verdict against which, in this colony, there is no appeal to law but only to His Excellency's clemency.' He paused, to be certain that the jury was fully attentive and nodded his head several times before continuing. 'The prisoner's crimes that led to his committal to Parkhurst were minor, petty theft in the main, the last resort of one so young abandoned to fend for himself in the appalling London slums ... never a violent act. Since his arrival here, he's borne in general a good character and shown signs of reformation.' He turned to the bench. 'I have no more to say, Your Honour.'

'You did well, Richard,' Schoales said as Nash resumed his seat.

'Not well enough, I suspect. The best we can hope for is clemency, I think.'

Mackie called for silence and said that the jury should retire to consider its verdict.

As Schoales left the court with Nash, he tried to overhear conversations among the people leaving the court, to gain some sense of any resolution of opinion, but could hear too little. They walked slowly to a bench under a tree in the gardens that were being established near the court. They were joined by William Brockman, one of the earliest settlers, who had a large holding at Herne Hill on the Swan River upstream from Guildford. He had been, for several years, a non-official member of the small Legislative Council that advised the Governor.

'A bad business, John,' he said. 'You can't expect there not to be at least one rotten egg in the basket. I must say that I'm pleased with the boy you assigned to me, Henry Wilson. He's been with me over a year now, and he's turned out well. I'd not be surprised if he took up land on his own in a few years.'

'By and large, that first batch have turned out better than the second,' Schoales said.

Brockman turned to Nash. 'You defended very well, Richard.'

Nash shook his head. 'I'm not hopeful.'

'If I have a chance, I'll speak to the Governor,' Brockman said.

'He'll feel obliged to stand by the verdict and Mackie's judgement,' Nash said. 'I believe you've engaged John to defend one of your farm workers.'

'Yes, Stoodley. He's charged with murdering one of the natives from the tribe up my way ... I don't know what to think of it, but I'm sure John'll defend him as well as you defended Gavin this morning.'

A bell was rung to signal that the court was reassembling.

16

There was almost no sound in the court as the members of the jury resumed their seats and waited some minutes for Mackie to return.

'I call on the foreman of the jury,' Mackie said. 'Have you reached a verdict?'

'Guilty as charged, Your Honour.'

There was a buzz of conversation in the court.

'Silence in the court,' Mackie said. 'Is your verdict without qualification?'

'We found no grounds for recommending mercy for the accused.'

'I commend the jury,' Mackie said. 'I consider your verdict the proper one, despite the able defence of my learned friend Mister Nash. Given the enormity of the crime, the penalty may seem inevitable. However, I wish to reflect before passing sentence. I reserve my judgement until the forenoon of tomorrow.'

When Mackie had left, Schoales asked, 'What do you think of Mackie adjourning, Richard?'

'I wouldn't count on any mercy. I think Mackie simply wants to show that he was not rushed into announcing a sentence that he's already determined.'

Gavin was returned to the Perth prison, but Schoales had no time to visit him, as the trial of Brockman's man Stoodley would begin after lunch. He asked a constable to tell Gavin that he would visit him later in the day.

The trial of Stoodley took less time than that of Gavin. It was alleged that he had gone looking for missing cattle which had either strayed or been driven off by natives. He came across a group of natives, both men and women, sitting around a fire near the huts where he and his fellow servants lived. Believing they may have stolen or killed the missing cattle, he lashed at them with a whip to drive them away. He could not speak their language and so could not communicate with them. Wabbemura, one of the men, resisted and threatened Stoodley with a cudgel. Stoodley struck him three times on the head with the handle of his whip, and the man fell senseless. His fellows carried him off into the bush. The natives reported the incident to a friendly settler, who led an investigating party to a new grave. The body was too decomposed to be identified positively. However, articles with the body were identified as belonging to Wabbemura.

The prosecution case was weakened because two of the witnesses gave conflicting evidence – one that Wabbemura menaced Stoodley, the other that he had only defended himself from attack. Schoales, still preoccupied with the morning's trial and his grave concern for Gavin, found it difficult to concentrate.

When he was called on to address the jury, he made an effort to focus on the details. He drew attention to the conflicting evidence and, feeling that he was parodying Richard's address to the morning jury, continued, 'The evidence against the accused is circumstantial. Although the body was claimed to be Wabbemura's, it was not identified positively. It's difficult to see how the charge could be laid. There's no proof that Wabbemura is dead or that, if he is, that he died of the alleged blows. You've seen the alleged weapon ... the whip. It's improbable that the native could have been killed by such a light weapon. It is notorious that natives assault each other often with their waddies without receiving fatal injury.'

Mackie addressed the jury briefly, advising them to consider the evidence as carefully as they would have if the victim had been a white rather than a native. The jury could consider a verdict of murder – a wilful act – or one of manslaughter.

After a short retirement, the jury found Stoodley not guilty.

Brockman came up to Schoales outside the Courthouse, to congratulate him. 'I'm obliged. Call on me at any time if I can be of service.'

'Thank you,' Schoales said. 'The occasion may arise sooner than we expect.' He stumbled.

Brockman grasped his arm, and said, 'Are you alright?'

'I'm exhausted.'

'I don't wonder,' Brockman said.

17

Because Gavin would not be sentenced until the morning, Nash decided to stay in Perth overnight. He had warned Elizabeth that this might happen, and had booked a room at Leeder's hotel that morning. It was a better class hotel than Strickland's, with a superior dining room. He invited Schoales to spend the evening with him and join him at supper. Schoales was glad to accept, dreading a night alone waiting for the verdict.

After Nash had confirmed his booking, he and Schoales walked westward along the Terrace and part way up Mount Eliza, where they stood quietly to watch a brilliant sunset.

'Red sky at night, shepherd's delight,' Nash said.

'I hope it won't be red in the morning ... shepherd's warning,' Schoales said, but immediately wondered if he was tempting fate by using the word shepherd.

'For heaven's sake, let go of it, John.' Nash turned to walk back. 'Let's go to the hotel for a drink before supper.'

A cold south-easterly wind freshened as they walked back, and they were glad to find a fire lit in the saloon. Nash ordered a half bottle of sherry and the two men took seats either side of the fireplace. Schoales was glad that there was no one he knew in the saloon; he did not want to talk about the trial. Two glasses of sherry warmed him and eased his mood, although he said little while they waited to be called to the dining room.

Nash ordered the roast beef, but Schoales asked for just two lamb chops with a small serve of vegetables. Nash called for a bottle of claret and the wine helped to ease Schoales's mood further. He managed to eat the meal, but without relish. He felt a little tipsy when they returned to the saloon, but accepted a glass of port. He dozed in his armchair for half an hour. Nash was reluctant to wake him, but did so at nine o'clock.

'Time for bed, I think, John. Would you like me to walk to the mill with you?'

'No, I'll be alright,' Schoales said.

His voice was a little slurred. Nash was not sure if it was the wine or his weariness.

Schoales lay down on his bed fully clothed. He felt nauseous, so he got up, and went to the bathroom to get a drink of water. He vomited into the basin. That eased his nausea. It also cleared his mind and he began to go over the events of the day, desperate to discover some hope in the outcome. He undressed slowly and, donning a nightshirt, returned to his bed.

18

Schoales had slept fitfully until daylight. When he got up and glanced out the window, he saw that the clouds in the eastern sky were bright red.

He returned to the Courthouse at nine o'clock in the morning with Nash. Mackie would pronounce sentence at a quarter past that hour. There were no troops on duty, and there were fewer people waiting to enter. Schoales took a deep breath as he entered.

Nash glanced at him anxiously. 'You look done in, John,' he said.

'I didn't sleep very well,' Schoales said.

'I'm not surprised. At least it will soon all be over.'

None of the Pollards were there. They had suffered enough, and Schoales felt that he could not have faced them.

Mackie entered slowly and placed his notes on the bench before sitting down. The people in the court were quiet. Mackie ordered Gavin to stand in the dock. The boy stood slowly and looked around the court calmly, apparently still unaware of what was happening.

'Prisoner at the bar,' Mackie said.

Gavin did not respond. A constable nudged him and pointed to Mackie.

'The jury has properly found you guilty of the foul deed of murder. I can see nothing in the case to recommend mercy, especially as you murdered one who had shown you friendship.

It was a heinous crime, without any provocation at all. It is lamentable that a boy so young should have committed one of the most diabolical crimes that the foul fiend could have instigated. I can only hope that you are aware of the solemnity of this occasion.'

'Mackie is,' Nash whispered.

'Are you aware that your hours are numbered, and that in a short time you will be in the presence of your Maker who alone may understand the dark processes of your heart? It would be some atonement for your foul deed if you were to make a full confession of the motive that influenced you to commit it.'

He waited. The constable nudged Gavin again, and the boy pushed the constable's arm away angrily.

'Prisoner at the bar,' Mackie said more loudly. Then, as Gavin still did not respond, he rapped the bench with his gavel and said, even more loudly, 'John Gavin.'

Gavin now focussed on Mackie.

'It is now my duty,' Mackie resumed, 'my unpleasant duty, to pronounce sentence.'

'The hypocrite, it's his big day,' Nash whispered.

Mackie placed a black cap slowly on his head. 'You, John Gavin, shall be taken to the gaol from whence you came and on Saturday next, the sixth day of the said month of April ...'

'My God!' Nash said, 'Easter Saturday. It's blasphemous.'

Mackie frowned at him, before continuing, 'You will be hanged by the neck until you be dead and afterward your body shall be hung in chains in such convenient place as the sheriff shall select ...'

Schoales tried to protest, but Nash stayed him.

'May Almighty God, for Jesus Christ's sake, have mercy on your sinful soul.'

The courtroom was hushed for a moment, and then there was a tumult of talk. Schoales could not understand its tone – some awe of the occasion and the sentence, some relief, some approbation. Or was he just reading into it his own confusion?

Gavin remained standing, raised one manacled hand slowly and scratched his cheek. He then looked toward the people in the courtroom, turning his head slowly, as if puzzled. He saw Schoales and nodded.

Schoales did not know how to respond.

A constable entered the dock, took Gavin by one arm, and led him away. There was little sound, as all eyes followed the stooped, shuffling figure.

Mackie rose, dismissed the jury and left the court.

Nash gripped Schoales's shoulder. 'Don't take it hard, John. I'm sure the boy's guilty, even if I feel doubt about the reliability of the sentence ... I hoped that Mackie had reserved sentencing to consider that. Now I'm sure it was more for effect. What did I say about theatre?'

'I'll call on Hutt this afternoon,' Schoales said.

'Mackie'll have gone to him now. Don't expect too much from Hutt. He'll feel constrained as to his freedom to act now in these matters, since he was reprimanded by the Colonial Office over his reprieve of that native.'

'I must see Gavin first.'

'Must you? It will only distress you. Come home with me tonight.'

'I should see to the lad's needs. I'll come on Saturday or Sunday . . . after it's all over.'

'Goddamn it! You're not planning to witness the hanging?'

'It's my duty!'

'I don't think so. It's in the hand of the law officers now!'

'I can't desert the poor wretch at this time,' Schoales said.

Before Nash could answer, Brockman overtook them. 'It's a wretched business. I thought Mackie might have been more merciful,' he said. 'He sounded pompous, and I doubt the boy understood a word of it.' He paused, shook his head, and added, 'That business of hanging in chains afterward is damnably medieval!'

The men walked on toward the Terrace.

'Which way are you going?' Brockman asked, intending to offer Schoales hospitality.

'To the lock-up to see Gavin. There's such little time. Then I should go to Hutt.'

Nash spoke angrily, 'Don't go to Gavin. You'll torture yourself.' He shook his head. 'I'm sorry, John, but I've a client to see. Come to us as soon as it's over.'

Schoales stopped and watched Nash walk away. 'I have to go, Brockman,' he said. 'Gavin may need something, and I should arrange for him to see a priest.'

'Who are you thinking of?'

'I'll ask Gavin. But probably Mister King . . . I don't know that Gavin'll have given any thought to it. They're saying that, although I know he's a Roman, I've prevented him being seen by a Roman priest.' He suddenly remembered Brockman's offer of help. 'I say, Brockman, you offered to help.'

'Yes. What can I do?'

'Witness my conversation with Gavin.'

Schoales said no more during the short walk to the lock-up. The two men were admitted to Gavin's cell, which was larger and less gloomy than the one at the Round House. Gavin sat on the edge of the narrow bunk, his head propped in his hands, as if he could no longer bear its weight.

'John! How are you?' Schoales asked, not knowing any other way to begin.

The boy's eyes appeared darker against the pallor of his face. Then, surprisingly, he looked up with a faint smile and, thrusting out one of his legs, said, 'They got me new boots.'

Schoales turned to Brockman, shook his head and said, 'He doesn't comprehend ... not yet. I'm going to appeal to the Governor, but I'm not hopeful.' He turned back to Gavin. 'Mister Brockman and I have come to ask if you need anything. Would you like to talk to someone, to a priest? It's said you're Roman Catholic.'

The boy did not answer at once. Schoales suspected that his mind was wandering. However, before he could speak again, Gavin spoke in a weak voice, which Schoales strained to hear.

'I think so, but it's so long – '

'John, it would be better to confess before ... before – '

'I don't know no one.

'The Reverend King?'

'He's seen me already.'

'Would you like to see him again?'

Gavin nodded.

'You'll be taken back to the Round House this evening. I'll

ride to Fremantle tomorrow and I'll stay there until ... I'll see you there.'

As they left, Schoales asked Brockman if he was satisfied.

'Of course! I'll speak to as many as I can ... don't count on a successful appeal though.'

'I've arranged to visit the Governor at two o'clock.'

'Join me for lunch ... at Strickland's, perhaps, or any-where else you'd prefer,' Brockman said.

'Leeder's, I think. It has better fare ... besides, it's further from the court. I don't feel like bumping into anyone who was at the court this morning.'

Schoales still had no appetite, and satisfied himself with a corned beef sandwich. The pungent pickles that dressed the meat made it easier for him to eat it. Although tempted, he refused wine.

'I should be fully sober when I see the Governor,' he said.

'What do you hope for?'

'A stay of execution to start with. It's almost blasphemous to have it scheduled for Easter Saturday.'

'I thought the whole business has been rushed,' Brockman said. 'What else?'

'Mercy. Richard is convinced that the boy is guilty, but feels that his guilt has not been proven beyond doubt.'

'I heard that a meeting of the Executive Council was called as soon as the verdict was known, so it has probably met already. It may be too late,' Brockman said.

'Why the haste? Couldn't they have waited until after the Holy Days,' Schoales said, his voice harsh with anguish.

'Has the boy confessed?'

'Not yet ... shows no sign of wanting to. However, I'll go with George King when he visits the lad. Perhaps he will confess then, when he realises what is to happen. It would be some relief for me if he would.'

'You can't take responsibility for this,' Brockman said. 'It's in the hands of the Executive Council now.' He glanced at the clock on the wall. 'I also have an appointment at two o'clock, and I've further to go than you.' He stood up and held out his hand, which Schoales gripped warmly. 'Don't forget to call on me if there's anything I can do. I appreciate what you've done for me.'

After Brockman left, Schoales decided to order a glass of wine after all. He felt in need of its stimulus as he prepared to meet the Governor.

19

Schoales arrived early at Government House, which was already deteriorating, the mortar and the soft bricks fretting. The Doric columns of the portico looked pretentious against the decaying brickwork. Hutt, a stickler for punctuality, admitted Schoales promptly. He was a tall man and often stood when talking to visitors, to reinforce his authority.

'I've no doubt you've come about this, Mister Schoales.' He waved a sheet of paper. 'It's the warrant for the execution. I've just signed it. It's set for eight o'clock, Saturday morning, at the Round House. A nasty business altogether.'

'Yes, Your Excellency. I've come to ask you to consider clemency for the wretched lad.'

'On what grounds?'

'I believe the defence raised sufficient doubt to make the verdict unsound.'

The Governor shook his head. 'I discussed it at length with Mister Mackie. He told me that Mister Nash mounted a spirited and ingenious defence, that the trial was fair, the verdict sound. The crime was monstrous and an example must be set. The Executive Council met an hour ago and agreed with the verdict.'

'But, sir! No boy of his age has been hanged at home for some years now. Parkhurst was established to treat young criminals more mercifully. Couldn't Mister Mackie have deferred sentencing until after Easter?'

'You accuse him of haste?'

'Some haste, yes.'

'I think haste might be a mercy in a case like this, and the Executive Council agreed.'

'But I'm appalled that the execution is set for one of the Holy Days ... it's even been suggested to me that it borders on the blasphemous.'

'I don't wish to discuss this further,' Hutt said. 'Don't think I like this, but the verdict stands. I have to have good legal grounds to grant a reprieve. The home authorities made that plain when they censured me for staying the execution of one of those natives who were to be hanged last year.'

'The lad was only a petty thief. He had no record of violent crime.'

Hutt flushed. 'No more, if you please, Mister Schoales.' He paused and brushed his hand across his forehead. 'One thing, though. The hanging in chains. I didn't support that ... I hear that it's to be abolished at home. The Executive Council agreed to disallow that portion of the sentence.'

'Thank you for that, Your Excellency. Just one other thing.'

'What?'

'They say that the boy's a Roman, and some are saying I've denied him the comfort of his priest. I heard they might appeal to you.'

'Have you?'

'I gave him a choice and he said that it didn't matter. He did so in the presence of Mister Brockman, who I invited to witness. I've proposed Mister King and the boy agrees.'

'I don't see how anyone can object, then.' Hutt waved Schoales away with the warrant.

Schoales returned to his office at the mill. He wondered whether he should dress formally when he attended the execution, so packed his best suit with his other needs for the next two days. On his way to the livery stable, he arranged for his case to be taken to the Crown and Thistle in Fremantle by a carrier.

He arrived at the hotel in the early evening, somewhat eased by the ride in the cool of the day, and arranged to have an early supper before calling on George King. He was hungry at last and ate well, and although he denied himself wine with the meal, he allowed himself a glass of port before setting out to walk up High Street to St John's. As he approached, he noticed that lamps were lit within, so he entered by the main door and saw King standing near the altar. Two women parishioners were arranging flowers in large vases, including Easter lilies.

King saw Schoales enter and walked up the aisle to greet him. 'It's good to see you, John,' he said. 'I just wish it was not such a desperate time for you. I got your message and am ready to give the poor wretch whatever comfort I can.'

'I knew that you would, George. We ought to talk about how we will deal with the boy tomorrow.'

'How is he?' King asked.

'He did not seem fully conscious of what is ahead of him.'

'I did send a message to the Governor, suggesting at least a stay until after the Holy Days.'

'I don't think he'd received it when I saw him this after-noon. He was quite resolute, and the Executive Council had already approved the ... all the arrangements, by the time I saw him,' Schoales said.

'Has he confessed?'

'No. I hope that you may help him to come to that,' Schoales said.

The two women approached, having finished their task. King thanked them and then suggested to Schoales that he join him at the altar for prayer.

They knelt together. King prayed silently for guidance. Schoales, less sure of his faith, felt that he could not.

When they rose, King said, 'Come over to the house. I'll ask Jane to make us some coffee and we can talk.'

'How is Jane?' Schoales asked.

'Her asthma's bad again ... You know, one of the reasons we came here was that the doctors back home thought that the climate here might help her. It hasn't, I'm afraid. I've begun to think of moving to one of the eastern colonies.'

Mrs King was sitting in the corner of the parlour, working on embroidery. Schoales asked if he could see the work, in which she had incorporated some of the colony's wildflowers, including the strange red and green flower that was called a 'kangaroo paw'.

'That's beautiful,' he said. 'The flowers look alive.'

Mrs King smiled. Despite the warm colour of the lamp-light, her lips were bluish, suggesting that she had not long recovered from one of her attacks.

King ushered Schoales into his study, where he lit the

lamp hanging over his desk. Schoales drew up a chair so that he could sit close to his friend.

'Do you think the boy's guilty?' King asked.

'I'm not sure. He's always denied guilt quite resolutely. The evidence was not in his favour, but not conclusive, and mainly circumstantial.' Schoales cupped his hands together as if there were something that he wished to grasp. 'Richard defended him well. Although he believed the boy was guilty, he thought there was enough doubt to allow clemency.'

'But that has not been granted,' King said, frowning.

Schoales shook his head. 'If the boy is guilty, it would be better for his soul if he could be brought to confess before ...' Schoales broke off.

'I'll try to bring him to it,' King said.

'I'm torn,' Schoales said. 'If he is guilty, I'd like to know, and I'd like to know his motive. If he goes to the gallows before I know, I'll feel that I've failed as his guardian.'

'John, don't flagellate yourself,' King said, shaking his head.

'Then I think of the Pollards,' Schoales said. 'They've suffered two tragic deaths so close together ... but, will the hanging of a boy give them relief? I think they're sure he did it.'

'I just don't know, John. Perhaps, in their immediate grieving they'll wish for such grim justice, but I hope that later they may find it in their hearts to wonder what drove the boy to this foul act.'

Jane brought the coffee and the two men were silent for a while.

'I plan to spend some time in prayer back at the church, John,' King said. 'I need guidance before tomorrow. Will you join me?'

'No . . . thank you, George. I'm desperately tired. I've not slept well these last few nights.'

'I'm not surprised. I hope you can sleep this night. You need . . . we both need to be strong in spirit.'

Schoales stood up. 'When I took on the task of being guardian to these lads, I thought I'd be able to help them all to lead good lives. I never thought it would come to this.'

King stood up and laid a hand on his friend's shoulder. 'When I became a priest, John, I too did not foresee a thing like this. Come to me as soon as you feel ready in the morning.' King raised his hand in blessing. 'God be with you.'

'Amen,' Schoales said.

Schoales felt unutterably weary as he walked back down High Street to the Crown and Thistle. He was glad to feel so, hoping that he would enjoy an unbroken sleep this night.

He did fall asleep almost as soon as he had gone to bed, but woke several times, feeling cold despite the adequate covers on his bed, and was late rising.

20

On Good Friday, the Reverend George King kept an early vigil in his beloved church, praying for guidance. He then rehearsed some of the prayers for the Easter services. There was a satisfying resonance in the church, and he heard the dying echo of his voice. He prayed again for his friend from college days, who had been so distressed last night, hoping that he was adequate to the task of being the ghostly adviser for the condemned boy.

He was deeply offended by the scheduling of the hanging for Easter Saturday, and regretted that the colony had no Bishop, who would have more authority to intercede with the Governor. He often felt that idealists – some said dreamers – like himself and Schoales should not have come to this sandy, blighted place. At least, now Easter had come, and cooler weather would follow, there would be relief from the torments of ophthalmia and the swarms of flies and fleas, which, in a letter home, he had called 'our Egyptian plagues'.

When he came out of the church, he saw carpenters erecting the gallows by the Round House at the end of High Street; a grim task for one of the Holy Days. The intense light in this colony, unlike the softer, often mist-veiled light of Ireland, enabled one to see some things too clearly. The gallows reminded him forcibly that his church, a house of redemption, stood at one end of High Street, while at the other stood a house of retribution.

Until his friend arrived, he joined his wife, Jane, who was gathering vegetables in the garden behind their bungalow. She stood and took several deep, slow breaths. He hoped she was not going to have an asthma attack.

'Come inside and rest while we wait for John,' King said, taking the basket from his wife's hands and leading her into the bungalow.

When Schoales knocked on the open door at ten o'clock, King called him in. Schoales found his friend, still seated beside his wife, who was prostrate on a sofa, talking to her gently to distract her so that her breathing would regain its normal rhythm. The colony had taken its toll of George, too. He had lost that youthful, almost feminine, pink-and-white complexion which had made him the butt of their fellow students' jokes at Dublin. When King stood, Schoales also noted that his tall, thin frame was now slightly stooped.

King ushered his friend into his study, where they both sat down.

'I'm troubled,' King said, 'that I've not attended a condemned person before ... a mere boy what's more. I'm not sure how to proceed. I prayed for guidance last night, and again this morning. I believe that the Holy Spirit will guide me through it.'

'I trust your judgement, George. But you should know that the papists claim that I denied the boy access to a comforter, and you know you've raised their ire by engaging so fiercely with Father Brady while he was here.'

'Thank goodness he's gone to Rome,' King said. 'Although

I hear he's arranging to come back with missionaries and some nuns from the Sisters of Mercy.'

'Surely the Roman congregation is too small here for so many religious.'

'He was active among the natives in New South Wales. No doubt he hopes to convert them here, too.'

Neither man spoke for a few moments.

'You said, John, that the boy had no record of violent behaviour.'

'There was no mention in the records sent to me, but they are sketchy at best. Sometimes even their age isn't given definitely. It would be easier for me if there were more information about their characters. It would guide me in my dealings with them. Gavin's religion was given as Roman, but I don't remember him showing any desire to attend church, even though he was held at the Depot for several months.'

'Did he ask for a spiritual comforter after the trial?' King asked.

'No. I offered it to him. I said that he could choose, but he was indifferent. Besides, the Round House is in your parish, and he said that he had already seen you. But he agreed to see you again.'

'I don't imagine it will be an easy task, John. But I will do my best.'

The two friends again sat in silence for a while.

Schoales was the first to speak. 'I'm deeply grieved for the Pollards. They're good people, and they've suffered two tragedies close together. They trusted me when they took on Gavin, and the lad seemed to be prospering with them.'

'Who are we to know the will of God?'

'I sometimes wonder if his writ can run here.'

King shook his head. 'Why shouldn't it?' he asked. He put his hand on his friend's shoulder. 'I'll help you bear this trial. We should go to the Round House.'

King donned his cassock and the two men left the house to walk slowly down the dusty, glaring High Street; neither was anxious to arrive too quickly at the Round House. They had to walk between the gallows and the empty stocks to reach the stairs. As the air was still, smoke from the nearby blacksmith's furnace now veiled the scene. The carpenters, who had nearly finished their work, chattered cheerfully.

The sheriff invited them into his office before they went to Gavin's cell. His blunt speech and manner hid his distaste for the task of organising the execution.

'There are arrangements I need to discuss with you, Mister Schoales.' He paused. 'Thank God the Executive Council has omitted the hanging in chains afterward.'

'I was much relieved, too. It would have been barbaric.'

The sheriff nodded. 'I'm worried that the boy's too light. He's lost more weight, I think, in these last few days. Even if I allow the maximum drop, I think his body's too light for a mercifully quick end. I plan to have weights tied to his feet.'

Schoales shuddered, although he appreciated the humanity of the grim-faced sheriff. 'Thank you, Mister Stone, for your concern.'

The sheriff led the two men to a cell and unlocked it. King had to bend low to enter. Two chairs had been placed in the cell, although there was little enough room. King laid his hand on Gavin's head, who had sat up on his bunk when the two men entered. Schoales wondered what the boy was thinking.

'Good morning, my boy,' said King. 'We've come to comfort you in your trouble. Please kneel with me.' He turned to Schoales. 'Join us, John,' he said.

There was scarcely room for the three of them to kneel together. As they knelt, Schoales heard the hammering of the carpenters outside, and wondered if Gavin knew what the noise was about. Blessedly, it stopped at last. Schoales was glad for the silence, although downcast by the thought that all was now ready. He was also pleased that, since this was Good Friday, blubber was not being rendered in the trypots on the beach below. There was enough to bear without that nauseating stench.

King spoke briefly, calling on God to forgive the boy. When he finished, he helped Gavin to rise and return to his bunk.

'Do you know where your parents are?' he asked. 'I could write to them.'

Gavin shook his head. It was a strangely dislocated movement. He had unbuttoned his shirt and his scrawny neck and prominent collarbones were exposed. Schoales flinched as he thought suddenly of a noose about that neck.

'You've only the future of your own soul to think about, then.' King gazed earnestly at Gavin. 'Mister Schoales has told me that you keep denying that you did this awful thing. However, as you approach your last night on this earth, you must prepare to meet your Maker shriven of any sin.' King wished that he did not sound so stiff. He was struggling to find a way to the heart and mind of the boy, but warmer phrases would not come to his tongue. 'If you are to find peace in the afterlife, John, you must confess all your sins. You were a thief, although Mister Schoales hoped that you had put that behind you. He had faith in you, when others didn't.'

Gavin nodded, but in a way that suggested that his neck was stiff. 'I'd've starved if I 'adn't.' In the dim light of the cell, his skin appeared translucent.

King placed his hand on Gavin's head again. 'I accept that as a confession of your thieving ... Dear Lord, as your son begged forgiveness for the thief on the cross, grant, I beg you, forgiveness for this troubled boy.'

King leant back in his chair and waited a few moments before speaking again.

'Think carefully, John. We read these words at a service on this Holy Day. O merciful God, who hast made all men, and hatest nothing that thou hast made, nor wouldest the death of a sinner, but rather that he should be converted and live.'

Schoales wished he had chosen a more apt collect; even if the boy confessed, he would not escape the gallows. He prayed silently that God would show him a way, and stood up briefly to flex each leg before sitting down again.

King spoke again.

'Did you kill George Pollard?'

'She laid it on me.'

'Did you?'

'No. I told 'em that.'

Schoales realised that all his muscles were tensed. He breathed deeply and tried to ease them.

Gavin leant back against the wall and his eyelids drooped.

King spoke to Schoales. 'The boy's exhausted. Let's leave him for now and come back later.' He turned to Gavin. 'Sleep if you can, and try to compose yourself. Mister Schoales and I'll come back later.'

21

The two men returned to the sheriff's office, and he offered them tea. They took the thick white china mugs and went to the stone wall along the cliff edge, out of sight of the gallows. They leant on the wall, side by side, looking at the sea. Schoales was glad of the heaviness of the mug; it was something solid to hold.

'John, you said the evidence against Gavin was strong, even though you think it was, in some measure, inconsistent.'

'Yes! As I said, I'd like to know the truth before he goes to the gallows.'

King looked anxiously at his friend. 'John. Have faith. My prayers will be for you, too.'

Although it was a sunny autumn day, it was cool, as a gentle sea breeze was blowing. The distant calls of children at a ball game, and the raucous quarrelling of seagulls over scraps around the trypots, were the only sounds in the peaceful scene. The two friends remained silent as they watched several families promenading along the beach from the whaling station to Point Marquis.

Schoales was troubled by the stark contrast between the families enjoying themselves on one side of the Head, and the work on the gallows going ahead on the other side. He supposed that it was now unlikely that he would have children. He had almost given up hope of finding a partner in the colony. Besides, he needed to have his affairs in better order before he could consider marriage. It seemed that he would not have the pleasure of nephews or nieces either. Elizabeth and Richard were disappointed that they had, so far, not been able to have children. They missed their family back home even more, and had begun to talk of returning there some time. If they did, he would go too. He could not bear the thought of remaining here alone.

King interrupted his thoughts. 'There are clouds out on the horizon. I wonder if rain will come.'

'It often does here, at Easter,' Schoales said. 'Perhaps it's the full moon that has some influence.'

'It's all so contrary here,' King said. 'I can't get used to Easter as an autumn festival – it seems to emphasise the Crucifixion rather than the Resurrection.'

'However, Easter might be further away from pagan spring festivals here,' Schoales said.

King smiled for the first time that morning. 'That's one way of looking at it,' he said. 'Perhaps, on the other hand, it might bring us closer to the primitive church.'

They lapsed into silence again. The breeze had faded and the warmth of the sun began to make them drowsy, melting away some of the dread and tension.

'George,' Schoales said, stepping back a pace or two from the wall. 'I've had strange thoughts about Gavin lately. You asked about his parents. I said there's not much in his record. It's almost as if he came out of nowhere, an alien being, generated in the humid womb of that ship ... the *Shepherd*. My God, there's irony in the name!' He paused. His ideas seemed outlandish to himself. 'It's almost as if he's from another planet. He's been here only half a year and has caused so much grief and anguish. Sometimes, when I've visited him in that cell, I've felt the presence of evil, yet I do not think the boy's evil in himself. Is he, perhaps, possessed?'

King touched him on the arm, now even more deeply concerned about his friend. 'Don't, John. They're dangerous thoughts. Shall we pray together?'

'I've not prayed for months, George. I think I'm losing my faith. Much here seems to deny it. I thought that it might be a new beginning, that we might feel closer to God where so much of his creation has not been brought under the dominion of man. Now, I sometimes wonder if our Christian God can inhabit uncivilised places.'

'It's certainly not the Garden of Eden, but it is his handiwork. We must talk more after it's over. Talk and pray together. We should go back to Gavin.'

As the boy was sleeping soundly when they returned to his cell, they thought that it was kinder to leave him, so planned to return in the late evening.

'Gavin's so thin and pale now,' Schoales said as they walked back up High Street. 'As the sheriff said, he's wasting away. If only the execution could be stayed, he might waste right away and not need to go to the gallows.'

'We can't escape the events of tomorrow now,' King said. 'We must steel ourselves for the night's ordeal. Do stop taxing yourself.'

They walked on in silence toward St John's. King increased his pace. Schoales thought that his friend hastened toward sanctuary, but he did not accept King's invitation to attend evening service, nor to join him and Jane at dinner.

'I need a long walk. If I feel like it, I'll dine at the inn.' He began to walk away, but turned back. 'Have you noticed, George, how lonely one can feel at sunset, especially here? Why, even the animals fall quiet. I don't like to watch the sun setting over the sea, even if the colours are often splendid. I know that, beyond the rim of that ocean, it will pass on to rise back home.'

'Perhaps Gavin will feel something of that this evening,' King said. 'It may open his heart.'

Schoales decided to walk along the beach to the south of the town. He called at the Depot on the way. Mrs Jenkins met him at the door and told him that the few boys who were staying there had gone out.

'I hope they've not gone near the Round House,' Schoales said.

'No, I think they went down to the river. One of the natives gave them a spear and they want to see if they can spear some fish. I told them that, if they do, I'll cook it for them tonight.'

'I'm glad. The gallows are nearly finished, and they make a grim sight. Tell them I said they are not to go near there tomorrow.'

'I don't think they will. Not one of them seems to have a good word for John Gavin.' She paused. 'It's a terrible thing, Mister Schoales ... for everyone involved I think.'

Schoales wished that people would not keep saying that, but he nodded. 'For everyone,' he said.

Mrs Jenkins backed into the room. 'Come in and I'll make you some tea or coffee. I've made a fresh batch of scones.'

'Thank you, but not now. I need a long walk.'

'Some sea air might bring some colour to your cheeks,' Mrs Jenkins said.

Schoales did not walk directly to the beach, as he did not want to pass the hull of the wrecked ship. It would remind him too strongly of the arrival of the boys after the stranding of the *Shepherd.* He was glad that no one was about, as he did not wish to speak with anyone.

As he walked southward along the beach, he tried to evoke scenes that would remind him of better times, to push all thoughts of the next day from his mind. He summoned visions of Ireland and wondered if the greens were as brilliant as they seemed in those visions. Perhaps he and Richard should have persisted in their efforts to be admitted to the bar in Dublin, but the 'real Irish' were now being favoured. He had once overheard someone refer to Anglo-Irish like him as 'bastard Irish'. Perhaps it was a pipe-dream to think of going back.

The sea breeze strengthened and he was glad that he was wearing his riding cloak. He stepped out briskly, silently counting his steps. The rhythm of his walking and counting distracted his thoughts. When he had walked a thousand steps, he turned back, feeling somewhat more at ease.

As the breeze was now strong, he hurried back and was glad to reach the shelter of houses under street lamps being lit. There was a fire in the dining room at the Crown and

Thistle, but there was no one he knew in the room. The few men there were probably farmers from inland.

His appetite was still modest. The sherry he drank before the meal, and the glass of wine he allowed himself during it, only stimulated it a little. He was reluctant to leave the warmth of the dining room after the meal, but he had to be at George's house by eight o'clock. Before leaving the hotel, he put on a pullover; the cloak alone would be insufficient guard against the chill of the coming night.

22

Schoales arrived at King's bungalow by quarter-past eight. King came to the door, carrying his cassock, which he donned before setting out. He sighed.

'I'm not looking forward to this night,' he said.

The moon was now high enough to light the street as they walked, again in silence, to the Round House. Its limestone walls glowed in the moonlight. The fire in the blacksmith's forge had been extinguished, and the smell of burning charcoal lingered, but the smoke had cleared. The sheriff met them at the head of the stairs.

'I was looking out for you,' he said. 'Gavin's been asking for you for the past half-hour. He won't eat, even though I've offered him some special food.'

He gave them an oil lamp to take to the cell. They were alarmed to see, by the lamp's dim light, that Gavin was lying on his hard, narrow bunk, shivering violently. Schoales gripped his shoulders. 'John! John! What's the matter lad?'

Gavin stammered, 'M-m-mister Sch-sch-schoales . . . I-I-I'm so c-c-cold!'

In fact, the cell was still warm; being on the western side, it had benefited from the afternoon sun. Schoales went to the sheriff for extra blankets. The sheriff accompanied him back to the cell, carrying a tray with a bottle of rum and three glasses on it. 'You may all need this,' he said.

King wrapped the boy in blankets and his shivering began to subside.

The sheriff looked at the boy and then spoke quietly, 'It's not earthly cold he's feeling. I've been told that, on the last night, they begin to feel the cold of the grave.' He handed the tray to Schoales. 'Don't stint yourself. I've a special allowance.'

The bottle and the glasses rattled when Schoales took the tray and put it down on the small table the sheriff had put just outside the door.

King told the sheriff to take away one of the glasses. 'I don't need it, thank you,' he said. 'You John, though, and the boy. It might be a blessing for the boy to be drugged against the terrors of this night and the morning. However, do not addle his mind before he's had occasion to open his heart.'

Schoales drank a small tot quickly. It was bitter, probably navy issue. He held a glass to Gavin's blue lips. The boy choked at first, but swallowed it all. His shivering stopped at last and, although the light was dim, Schoales saw a faint flush of colour in his cheeks.

'Do you know the Lord's Prayer, John ... Our Father?' King asked the boy.

'I've forgotten.'

'Well, say it after me. You too, John, please.' He recited the prayer slowly, noticing that his friend's voice was not much steadier than Gavin's. Then he addressed the boy. 'John, we'll stay as long as you need us ... until you've unburdened yourself. You might sleep then. Your time is near, lad. This is your last chance to prepare yourself.'

'When will it be?' the boy asked.

'In the morning, at eight o'clock.'

'The morning? Tomorrer? Will it be quick?'

'I'm sure. The sheriff – he's a good man – has taken great care with all ... all the preparations.'

'Could I 'ave a little more of the rum?'

'Give him just a little, John.'

After swallowing the drink, more readily this time, Gavin slumped back and remained silent. He appeared to sleep for a quarter of an hour. Schoales was amazed at King's apparent calmness. He saw that his friend's lips moved as he prayed silently, and wished that he could join him, to make the time pass.

Schoales heard the call of an owl, and dogs barked occasionally. He stood up and walked out of the cell and once around the courtyard. There were no sounds from the other cells, although several of them held prisoners. The silence was eerie. When he returned, King touched his lips, signalling that Schoales should not speak. He gestured toward Gavin, who was now sitting up.

Gavin yawned. He began to mumble, but neither of the men could understand anything. In a little while they made out a few puzzling words: 'Buzzin' ... 'ornets ... layin' it on me.'

The boy dropped his head on his chest and remained silent for a few minutes.

'How long should we stay?' Schoales asked. 'He seems to be passing beyond our help. Either he didn't do it or he'll not tell us if he did.'

'Be patient, John. I think he's at a crisis. Those ramblings may come to something when his mind clears.'

Schoales wondered again at the resoluteness of his gentle friend. Was he, in his own way, possessed, but with God rather than the devil? He lost track of the passage of time, fidgeting frequently to ease his tensed muscles.

At last, Gavin woke and sat up. The blankets slipped from him but he did not begin to shiver again. He looked at King and Schoales in turn, but his eyes did not focus on them. Schoales stood up and opened the door, as the air was almost too foetid to breathe, but, as there was now no wind, there was no relief in the cell. King again gestured to him to remain silent.

When Gavin spoke his voice was barely audible. 'Mister King!'

'Yes, my boy.'

Schoales bent forward to listen, disappointed that Gavin had turned to King and not to him.

'Is it mornin' yet?'

'No, still the middle of the night.'

'I didn't mean to 'urt George ... not 'im.'

'Can you tell me more?'

Schoales tensed. King touched him on the arm, then leant forward and whispered, 'Say nothing, let the boy speak. A question might divert his mind.'

'I 'it 'im when 'e woke up when I went fer the adze.' Gavin's speech became incoherent again: 'Terrible buzzin' all the time ... to get the adze ... George woke up.' He leant against the wall beside his bed, and his head bent down as if he might be falling asleep again.

Schoales held his breath. The boy's confession was not enough; he must reveal his motive, too.

King stood up and stretched wearily, yawning. It was the first sign he had given of strain. 'It was some sort of confession. We'd better leave him to sleep while he can. It'll be a mercy if he can sleep away the night. We'll come back early in the morning.'

Schoales rose slowly from his chair. His limbs were stiff again from tense sitting for so long. Before he left, he pulled the blankets up to Gavin's chin. He stooped to pick up the tray with the bottle and the glasses, before joining King outside the cell. A lamp still shone in the sheriff's office. Schoales entered and returned the tray to him.

'Thank you for this,' he said. 'It helped the lad, I think, and me. You should know that he's just confessed, in a rambling sort of way, but we still don't know his motive. He's sleeping now. Mister King and I'll return early in the morning.'

'I'll be here early, too. I'll be glad when the awful business is done.'

'Thank God it won't be long,' Schoales said. He wiped his forehead with the back of his hand, surprised to find it moist, even though the night was cool.

King and Schoales bade the sheriff goodnight and left the prison. They stood side by side for several minutes at the head of the stairs. The white limestone walls of the town shone in the full light of the paschal moon, which, Schoales was surprised to see, was nearing the zenith. He had lost track of time in the cell.

A distant rooster crowed and was answered by one near at hand. Somewhere a dog bayed and was answered by others. From the tall trees near the swamps at the rear of the town could be heard the beautiful carolling of magpies. An owl perched on the crossbeam of the gallows standing to the left. The rope had been attached. The owl took off soundlessly and swooped down toward the scrub to pounce on some small nocturnal animal, which squealed when the talons closed on it.

Schoales shivered. 'There's a chill in the air, tonight, George.'

King wondered at the remark. In his cassock, he felt warm.

Schoales was exhausted and, when he returned to the inn, he took off his coat. He had walked quickly to the hotel, so that his shirt and underwear were dampened with sweat. He loosened his collar, lay down on the bed, and fell asleep as if he had fainted. His sleep was troubled by scenes of Gavin in his cell. He woke an hour later, got up and opened the window. There was a light breeze from the sea, which chilled him, as his shirt was still damp.

He undressed, and threw his clothes over the armchair, but did not bother to don a nightgown before returning to bed. He slept fitfully until he rose at half-past-five. His hand shook when he shaved, and he nicked himself twice. He decided to dress formally, in a dark suit. He fumbled with the buttons of his shirt and with the studs as he attached the stiff collar, which seemed tighter than usual around his neck.

He had absolutely no appetite for breakfast and felt slightly nauseous.

23

When Schoales arrived at St John's, King was emerging from the church, where he had gone early to pray. Schoales was surprised to find him apparently calm. King grasped both of his friend's arms and looked at him intently.

'You look fatigued, John. I hoped the boy's confession, as far as it went, would ease your mind, at least a little.'

'A little, yes, but I didn't sleep well. I had a nightmare when I did, and I woke when the gallows appeared in it.'

'I was troubled by images of the cross,' King said. 'I feel it's a sacrilege that this day was chosen.' He sighed. 'We should return to the boy. He'll need more comfort than us.'

'I'd still like to know his motive,' Schoales said.

'It may have been a moment's passion, not a conscious act. I doubt if the boy is fully sane. He may not know himself, or if he does, perhaps he can't explain. Even people like us don't find it easy to express our innermost thoughts.'

After a cup of coffee – neither felt like food – they walked slowly and in silence to the Round House. A group of spectators had gathered already near the end of High Street, where two soldiers prevented them going nearer to the site of the gallows.

Mr Jones, the tailor, was one of the group. He doffed his hat uneasily to Schoales and King, as if he was embarrassed to be found there. Others also turned away after bidding the two men good morning. One or two choked on the word 'good'. Some muttered that they had chanced upon the gathering, not aware of its purpose, and twirled their hats in their hands. Two men from the newspapers were busy taking notes.

Preparations near the gallows were well advanced. The slack of the rope was draped over the crossbeam. The noose hung down, not moving, as there was no breeze. A man backed a horse into the shafts of a small green dray beneath the gallows, on which a platform a few feet high had been erected. Six scarlet-jacketed soldiers stood at guard on the perimeter of the small level space. One of them raised the upper plank of the stocks and let it drop with a bang, laughing as he did so. Many roosters of the town crowed and many dogs bayed or barked. These familiar morning sounds seemed out of place this day. Schoales forced himself to look away. He was breathless when he and King reached the head of the stairs.

The sheriff greeted them in his office, just within the prison gate, solemnly and gruffly. 'Good morning, gentlemen. Everything's ready. The bell will begin to toll a few minutes before eight o'clock . . . I plan for it to be over in a few minutes.'

Schoales and King went to the cell. Gavin was awake, seated on his bunk with his blankets draped over his shoulders. The air in the cell felt damp and smelt of the sea. Schoales left the door wide open.

'Did you sleep, John?' Schoales asked, wondering if there was anything he could say that would not be banal. Should he be solemn, or try to cheer the lad?

King asked Schoales and Gavin to kneel with him and

they were forced together in the confined space. Gavin's breathing was laboured, and there was a sickly smell of nervous perspiration. Schoales was not sure if it was his or the boy's. King still appeared surprisingly calm. He had chosen to read the first collect for Easter Eve.

'Grant, O Lord, that as we are baptised into the death of the blessed Son our Saviour Jesus Christ, so by continual mortifying our corrupt affections we may be buried with him; and that through the grave, and gate of death, we may pass to our joyful resurrection; for his merits, who died, and was buried, and rose again for us, thy Son Jesus Christ our Lord, Amen.'

Schoales did not hear the collect as an expression of hope and redemption. His mind had grasped the phrase, 'by continual mortifying', and worried it, as a terrier a rat.

When King had finished, they all stood up, the men fumbling to shift their chairs. Gavin sat down on his bed and, looking toward the men, was dazzled by the morning light on the opposite wall of the courtyard.

He began to speak slowly. 'She was always layin' things on me . . . I could do nothin' right.' He clutched his head as if it ached. 'It's like a swarm o' bees . . . in me 'ead.'

He began to speak more rapidly, not always coherently, and told how he had taken the adze from the barn, planning to attack Mrs Pollard when she was asleep after lunch. He had hidden it under George's bed.

'When I went back for it, I didn't know George'd be there. I found a bit of wood instead, but she was awake . . .' He stopped and the two men thought that he might fall into a coma as he swayed back, but he shook his head and placed his hand over his ears. 'Bees ... or 'ornets ... it's all buzzin'!' He waved his hands wildly as if to fend off a swarm. 'I came back and George was still asleep. I dragged it out ... the adze ... but George woke up. I knew 'e could've taken me ... so I 'it 'im in the face ... He fell back ... I 'it 'im on 'is 'ead ... again ...'

Schoales and King waited again tensely. The smell in the cell was now nauseating, but they could not leave yet. Schoales found that he was holding his breath and forced himself to breathe.

'I called George,' Gavin continued. 'I called 'im ... but 'e was dead. I dropped the adze and ran ... ran ... the 'ornets were after me.' He fell back on the bunk.

King spoke quietly to Schoales. 'We should not plague him with more questions. You know the motive now. He has confessed as much as he can. Let him sleep.' He drew out his watch and sighed. 'Only half an hour now! You go outside, John. I'll stay and pray for the poor wretch's soul. He'll soon be in God's hands. Leave a glass of the rum with me ... it would be a mercy if he was numbed.'

Schoales half filled a glass and handed it to King. As he did so, Gavin sat up again.

'I ran to the river,' he said. 'I tried to drown meself ... it was too shaller ... too cold ...' The rest was unintelligible rambling.

King spoke to Schoales. 'I think his mind has turned finally. It may be a mercy.'

Schoales left the cell. Early sunlight now lit the courtyard brightly, and he sank onto the edge of the well. Pale faces watched him through the grilles of other cell doors, making him uncomfortable, so he walked out of the prison. The horse was now secure in the shafts of the dray, and had been given a nosebag to keep it quiet. The sound of it munching chaff was unusually loud; every other creature had fallen silent. There was a pungent smell from a steaming heap of horse dung. A ladder was propped against the dray, and another against the platform on the dray. He turned away, feeling nauseous again, and walked around the prison to the sea wall along the other side of the Head, where he would wait out of sight of the final preparations.

Now feeling numbed, he stared out over the sea toward the low, blue silhouettes of the islands, which marked where the colony ended and the empty waste of the ocean began. Although he knew the lad's motive, he still paced uneasily backward and forward alongside the wall. Before he became Guardian of Juvenile Immigrants, he had walked here often. In the summer, he had sometimes bathed in the sea below. The men and boys bathed at this end, the women and girls at the southern end. He had often stood by this wall to see a ship arrive with news of home. At other times, he had watched the whalers at their preparations. Once, he had seen them catch a whale in the bay. He had felt pity for the huge beast as it writhed in the water for some time before the whalers could administer the coup de grâce. By then, the sea about it was scarlet.

He wondered if he would ever be able to come to this place again, and doubted that, if he did, he would ever feel comfortable there.

24

When the prison bell began to toll, Schoales returned to the cell, where the sheriff waited with two constables. Gavin stumbled and blinked as King led him out.

Gavin glanced at the sheriff. 'Does it 'urt to be 'anged?' he asked.

The sheriff spoke gruffly. 'No lad. It'll be very quick.'

He began to move away from the cell, but Gavin stopped and, stooping, began to unlace one of his boots.

'No need to do that, lad.'

'I don't want me new boots to be spoilt.'

Schoales stooped to help the boy. 'At least allow him this,' he said. When he had removed the boots, he placed them on the wall around the well.

A prisoner in one of the cells began to beat a metal plate against the grille of the door in time with the bell.

The sheriff called a warder and spoke angrily. 'Stop that man and confiscate anything in the cells that could make noise. Warn them that if they shout, I'll charge them with rioting.'

He turned back to the small party and led the way out of the prison. The constables walked on either side of the boy, and Schoales and King followed close in the rear. There was a stir among the spectators when the party emerged through the gateway, and began to descend the steps in front of the prison.

Gavin winced when he stepped on a sharp piece of stone as the party walked to the head of the stairs that led down to the lower ground. For a moment, his heart lifted when he saw the bright morning and the scarlet jackets of the soldiers. Something stirred deep in his memory: a green lawn, men in scarlet coats, sounds of fife and drum, and a shadowy figure, a woman standing beside him and telling him that they were old soldiers from the French wars. Then he saw the gallows. One masked man stood at the front of the dray below the gallows, while another, on the dray, adjusted the noose. The man by the head of the horse removed its nosebag and the horse tossed its head and snorted impatiently.

When they reached the foot of the stairs, Gavin stumbled and would have fallen if Schoales had not caught him in his arms. The boy trembled violently.

'Me legs . . .' he gasped, 'I can't walk. Can you carry me?'

Schoales glanced at the sheriff, who nodded, so Schoales picked up the boy and, surprised to find him so light, carried him to the foot of the ladder by the dray and helped him up. The two masked men hauled the boy up and dropped a hood over his head before hoisting him onto the small platform below the noose.

Schoales turned away and walked toward the entrance to the Whalers' Tunnel. He was only half aware of King's voice, beseeching God to forgive the boy, although he pitched it loudly enough for the spectators to hear. He heard one phrase clearly, before he entered the tunnel: 'being put to death in the flesh, but quickened by the spirit.'

On the platform, Gavin winced as the men roped weights

to his ankles. Then one of them dropped the noose over his head. Gavin felt the rope and began to gasp for breath. His chest heaved, and his legs began to buckle. One of the masked men held him upright.

The sheriff signalled to the man who held the horse. The man slapped it and urged it forward. The platform began to slide forward under the boy's feet, and the hangman released him. His body canted as the weights dragged to the edge of the platform.

When the hooded body dropped, seagulls on the wall above were startled and fluttered away in noisy alarm. Their cries mingled with what sounded like a loud sigh from the spectators. The bell stopped tolling.

A constable fetched Schoales. As he emerged from the tunnel, blinking in the bright light, he glanced toward the gallows, where Gavin's body turned slowly on the rope. The horse and dray were led away. The soldiers, ordered to stand easy, shuffled to ease their muscles. The spectators dispersed silently. Schoales wondered what else they had expected to see, other than the sight of the frail body, jerked to a halt at the end of the rope.

Schoales shuddered, wondering if the sudden chill was in his body or his spirit, and whether it would ever leave.

The sheriff was grim faced. 'A nasty business, Mister Schoales ... not as quick as I'd hoped, but I think he didn't suffer.'

'Thank you, Mister Stone, for ... for all that you did. I'm deeply obliged and I'll say so in my report.'

'The troops'll remain on guard. I'll have the body cut down and taken back to the cell. I'll arrange for a decent canvas shroud. There's a sailor here in prison for deserting ship. He says that he's made shrouds. Oh, and another thing. Mister Harris, the surgeon, has asked if he can take a death mask and a mould of the head.'

'Whatever for?'

'I believe he wishes to send them home to the Royal College of Surgeons.'

'I think it's ghoulish, but I've no objections. When will the body be ready for burial?'

'Come back about three o'clock. I hope there'll be few about then.'

Yes,' Schoales said, 'I'd rather the burial be unobserved.'

'The troops'll stay and keep people away from the site. I'll have a grave dug between the dunes.'

'Thank you again.'

Schoales went to King and they grasped hands.

'I believe the boy was prepared at the end, John,' King said. 'He's in the hands of his Maker now, and I hope he'll find peace at last. Come to me when you wish ... when you're ready to talk. I must go now ... I have a service to conduct. I pray I'll never have such an Easter again.'

Schoales returned to the inn and tried, without success, to rest alone in his room. He had no appetite for lunch, and returned to the stables to fetch his horse. He rode far south along the beach, past the last of the houses, scarcely conscious of time or space. He doubted if there would ever come a time when he would not be haunted by the scenes of the morning. He could still not make up his mind whether to resign. He would talk it over with Elizabeth and Richard and see if they had given any further thought to quitting the colony.

When he returned to the Round House, dark clouds were moving in from the sea. He went to the sheriff's office.

'The shroud's been done, but I told the sailor to leave the final closing until you've identified the body,' the sheriff said.

Schoales walked slowly to the cell. Gavin's body, in its neatly stitched canvas shroud, lay on the bunk. Although the canvas was heavy and tar-stained, the stench of urine and faeces seeped through. The head, which was set at an even more grotesque angle, had been left uncovered for the taking of the casts. There was a rope burn on the neck. The skull, the hair clipped for the casting, was still smeared with plaster, the lips white with it. He remembered Mrs Pollard saying that Gavin's lips were white with cream when she found him in the kitchen.

He could find no cloth handy, so took out his white linen handkerchief and asked a warder to bring some water. He wiped away as much of the plaster as he could and then went, absent-mindedly, to return the handkerchief to his pocket, but checked himself. He stared at it for a while and then stuffed it in the shroud. He called the sailor to complete the stitching and sent a warder to tell the sheriff that he was ready for the burial party.

The sailor was a Cornishman, squat and dark. He whistled

cheerfully while he deftly closed the shroud with a sail needle and stout twine.

Two prisoners, under the guard of two warders, carried the shrouded corpse to the grave and lowered it in gently, as Schoales had ordered them. Schoales cast a handful of sand onto the canvas. He would have liked to perform some rite, but none was allowed. The words that King had read at the foot of the gallows would have to suffice. After a long pause, he ordered the grave to be filled in, and the area swept as the party retreated, to obliterate any signs of digging and all their footprints. The storm clouds were nearer, so rain might wash away all traces of the grave.

25

Schoales went to the Depot and asked Mrs Jenkins to make him strong tea, but declined any food.

The bitterness of the tea mixed ill with the bile that had risen to his mouth. When he tried to swallow, he retched and put the cup aside.

'How've the lads taken it?' he asked Mrs Jenkins.

'Quiet ... no larking about. But none of them seemed to have much time for Gavin.'

'No, the poor devil.' Another spasm wrenched his stomach.

'Are you ill, sir?'

'I'd rather not go through that again. Where are the lads now?'

'They've gone off somewhere with a ball and bat. I told them on no account to go near the Round House. They're probably down by the old hulk on the beach. It's their favourite playground. They sometimes play at pirates, I think ... Robinson's here, though, Edward. He calls himself Ned now.'

'Why's he here?'

'He walked down from Guildford, as I understand, but he's in such a state I can't get much sense out of him.'

'Damn it, I thought he was settled with the Austins, but if he's absconded again, they won't want him back. Send him to me.'

When the boy arrived, Schoales thought that he was

unhinged again, but he spoke severely to him. 'I don't know what to do with you, boy, but you've got to learn.' He took down a cane that he kept on top of one of the cupboards and ordered the boy to bend down. The boy whimpered, and collapsed to the ground, pulling his knees to his chest.

Schoales dropped the cane and left the room. He found Mrs Jenkins in the kitchen.

'There's nothing we can do for such a boy. No one will want him if he keeps absconding, especially as he then lapses into filthy habits again. I'm afraid he'll be a trouble for you, but I've got much to do before I go ...' He paused, feeling a sudden chill again. 'I'm going to my sister's place, perhaps for a week.'

'You work too hard, sir,' Mrs Jenkins said.

'I plan some changes that might ease the load. I'll tell you about them next time I come.'

Schoales's legs ached as he walked to fetch his horse again from the stables; his muscles had been tensed too long in the morning. When he was astride, he had a view over the low scrub of some of his lads playing happily around the old hulk, no doubt free of work this day. He called one over.

'Tom, please take a note for me to Mister King at the church.'

He was not ready to see George, but what excuse could he give? He heard the sound of thunder approaching from the west. He should waste no time if he was to be back in Perth before the storm came. He wrote a note on a page from his notebook:

Dear George, I am sorry but I must excuse myself. I wish to be back in Perth before the storm. I will come down after I return from Elizabeth's. John.

He tore out the page, gave it to the boy, and then turned his horse toward the ferry. Across the river, on high ground, he looked back toward the Round House. At this distance, and with the dark clouds casting a shadow, he could not see the gallows, but the signal mast stood out like a frail cross against the leaden sea. His horse fidgeted, uneasy at the sound of thunder.

He decided that he could not now give up his post. It would seem as if he was running away.

26

Schoales sat at his desk, fiddling with pens and folding large sheets of blotting paper to a more convenient size. He feared he had caught a chill, as he had been soaked by the rain on his return from Fremantle. He had been exhausted after the ride and had slept for an hour in an armchair in his wet clothes. When he woke, he had stripped off his clothes and let them fall on the floor, and began to shiver violently. Although he put extra blankets on his bed it was some time before the shivering stopped. He then slept restlessly, finally waking at nine o'clock. His mouth was sour from a glass of whisky he had drunk soon after rising, and he had not eaten. He wanted to write his report to the Governor, so that he could leave it with him on Monday morning. He finally took up a pen and began to write:

It has become my melancholy duty to report to Your Excellency the death of Government Juvenile Immigrant John Gavin. The event took place on Saturday morning last at 10 Minutes past 8 at Fremantle by the exception of the Court of Quarter Sessions on my unfortunate ward for the murder of the son of his master, George Pollard.

He swore and flung the pen against the stain on the wall near the fading inscription, HERE BE DRAGONS. Ink spattered on the whitewash. He went to the window and forced it open. The storm had passed, leaving the air washed and sparkling, but he could not shake off his depression.

He gave a brief account of Gavin's confession, which, so written, seemed much more cogent than the boy's ramblings. He was about to sign the report, when he added a final paragraph:

To the High Sheriff and his assistants I return my thanks for their excellent arrangements and hearty acquiescence in any suggestions proposed for the amelioration of the boy's suffering. And I trust that neither my lot nor theirs be so cast as to subject us to the repetition of such an awful duty.

He picked up his letter book, which contained copies of his previous reports, and turned back to his report on the boys who had caused trouble during the voyage of the *Shepherd*:

The probation in Parkhurst as far as I can perceive is amply suffi-cient to reclaim a lad whose course of crime has not been of long duration, but a reference to my conduct book shows, that where a boy has been in crime for two, three, or more years even the disci-pline of Parkhurst, admirable as it is, is not sufficient to wean him thoroughly from his habit of Sin. Take the following cases from the lads per Shepherd

    1. John Kirk . . . . two years a pilferer
    2. Levi Green 2   "   "   "
    3. Joseph Lenon 3   "   "   "
    4. William Porter . . . . 2½ "   "   "
all concerned in a deep & well contrived robbery on board ship
    5. John Gavin . . . . many years a thief

He picked up a pencil, scored through 'many years a thief', and wrote above it, 'hanged for murder'.

It was midday by then, and he knew that he should try to eat. While he was preparing some sandwiches, Richard Nash arrived.

'I was worried about you,' he said. 'Where were you this morning?'

'Here. Why?'

'Did you forget the special Easter service this morning? You were missed from the choir.'

Schoales thumped his forehead. 'I'm sorry. I'd a bad night and woke late.'

'I'm not surprised. I told them where you were yesterday, and they were shocked. Missus Symmons, in particular, asked me to say how she felt for you.'

'I had to write this report for the Governor, too.' Schoales gestured to the papers on his desk.

Nash picked up a glass, which was on the desk, and sniffed it. 'It's too early to be drinking spirits,' he said.

'I caught a chill.'

'You look ghastly, but watch it. Strong spirits can give false comfort.' He put down the glass. 'Why don't you come back with me now, instead of waiting until tomorrow?'

'I may not be able to come tomorrow, after all. I've an appointment with the Governor at nine o'clock, and then I must go to the Depot.'

'For God's sake, why?'

'A problem with one of the lads, Robinson, a sad case I've told you about. He absconded from Austin's. I went to a lot of trouble to place him; he was the last of the *Shepherd* lads to be assigned. He turned up at the Fremantle Depot on the day ... on Saturday.'

'He sounds hopeless.'

'I'm afraid I lost my patience with him ... was going to cane him, but he fell into a pitiable heap and I couldn't ... but we've no asylum I can commit him to here. I'm at my wits end.'

On Monday morning, Schoales was ushered immediately to the Governor, who glanced up when he entered.

'Ah, Mister Schoales. Please sit down. You look exhausted, and I'm not surprised. I felt troubled enough, but you bore the brunt of it.' He picked up a paper. 'I've just read this despatch from the sheriff. I understand that it was done as quickly as possible.'

'It was, and I've come to deliver my own report. You'll see that I commend the sheriff especially ... he might have had the worst of it.'

The Governor took the report and placed it on top of some other paper. 'Thank you. I can't say I'll enjoy reading it. Now take that leave you asked for. Try to put this behind you, and turn your mind to the other lads under your care.'

'I've some ideas for the few incorrigibles, like Edward Robinson, who's in trouble again. Mister Austin won't have him back, so I'll have to cancel his indentures and take him back into care.'

'No more for now. Come to me afterward.'

Schoales left for Fremantle as soon as he had left Government House, arriving at the Depot at midday. He found Mrs Jenkins having her lunch in the kitchen and she offered him food, which he was glad to accept, although he managed only a slice of bread and some cold meat.

'How's Robinson?' he asked.

Mrs Jenkins looked distressed as she spoke. 'He told me why he walked down on Saturday.'

'I doubt it's a good reason.'

'You remember me telling you that he and Gavin were thick, when they were here together. He told me that someone told him that Gavin was to be hanged.'

'You don't mean?'

'I do. That's why he was here. He left Mister Austin's on Friday and slept beside the river ... he got to the Round House in the morning ... I think he saw it, but he won't say.'

Schoales knew, then, that his chill was in the spirit. It was some moments before he spoke. 'I'll talk to him next time I'm here. He needs to be in a better mood. I'm sorry you've got care of him again.'

He called at the mill to collect what he needed, before setting out for Guildford, and arrived at Elizabeth's house at sunset.

Elizabeth embraced him. 'You look done-in,' she said. 'Richard was very concerned when he saw you yesterday.'

'I never want to go through that again,' Schoales said. 'And I think I caught a chill on the way back from Fremantle in the rain. A little fever, but it's easing, I hope.'

'It'll do you good to do nothing for a while. But go in. Gerald's there with Richard.'

Lefroy stood up and grasped Schoales by the arm as he entered the parlour. 'I'm sorry for what happened,' he said.

Schoales wished that people would not keep reminding him.

'It's always good to see you, Gerald,' he said. 'Still courting the fair maid of Sandalford?'

Lefroy smiled. 'I think I might be more in favour than de Burgh at present ... but I must be patient for a few years yet.'

'Have you found that land you're looking for?'

'No, but I think I may find it up north near the Moore River. I'm going up to look again in May. You should join me.'

'Not this time, but I might be able to another time if it fits in with one of my trips checking on the lads ... I hope things will ease up.'

Elizabeth entered and spoke crossly. 'John, I told you to forget about your work for a few days.' She turned to Lefroy. 'You should take him in hand, Gerald, when you can spare time from Sophie.'

'There are plenty of ducks on the river. What about tomorrow morning?' Lefroy asked.

Over the following days, Schoales began to relax and looked fit again when he left.

As he was riding away, Elizabeth turned to Nash and said, 'I wish John could find a wife.'

'He won't court young girls, like Gerald, and there are few suitable single women in the colony. Perhaps, when more families arrive, he may find someone. However, I'm glad to see he seems to be in better shape. I was really worried when I saw him on Sunday; he'd been at the whiskey early. I hope he won't look for comfort that way.'

'How can you think that, Richard?'

Nash put his arm around her shoulders. 'He drank modestly while he was here, so we needn't worry. I urged him again to give up his post and join me in the law work.'

'Did he agree?'

'Not yet. He says if he resigned now, he'd feel like a deserter.'

Elizabeth put her hand up to her shoulder and touched her husband's hand. 'I begin to wonder if we should have come here.'

'Don't forget that Irish nationalism was making it more difficult for John and me to find work ... one day, though, I would like to go back.'

27

Schoales was able to return to his work on Monday, with more energy after his short break at Elizabeth's. He had no pressing engagements, so worked methodically to get on top of deskwork.

On Wednesday, he went to the Depot at Fremantle to check on Robinson. Mrs Jenkins said that the boy was calmer but still fouling his clothes.

'I'd better see the boy. Send him to me.'

When Robinson entered the room, he was clutching both his shoulders, with his arms crossed on his breast and his head dropped so that his chin rested on them. He stank.

'What am I going to do with you, Edward ... or is it Ned, now?' Schoales asked. 'I thought you were happy with Mister Austin, and he was a kind master.'

'Mister Pomeroy was kinder.'

'But he couldn't keep you there. Perhaps he might be able to later, when he needs a boy all the time. What troubles you, Ned?'

The boy did not speak for a few moments. When he did so, he raised his head only a little, and spoke in not much more than a whisper. 'I can't help it,' he said, 'voices ... gettin' at me ... kill yerself.'

Schoales grasped one of the boy's wrists. There was a new, healed scar on it.

The boy drew back. 'Don't beat me,' he pleaded.

'Not if . . . no, I'll try other ways.'

Schoales now saw no hope for the boy. He had thought that, if he could save him, he would not feel so guilty about Gavin.

Next day, back at the mill, Schoales drafted yet another memorandum to the Governor about Robinson. His hand was a little unsteady as he wrote:

The Devil who prompts such a suggestion may as readily suggest the murder of another person, and after the awful example of the promptitude with which such a suggestion may be adopted even against a warm friend, what may I not fear if a boy of this temper should feel against or hurt by the conduct of his master toward him. With Your Excellency's consent I trust not to be made to re-assign the boy – I declare him unfit for any situation, and I hope Your Excellency will transfer the boy back to Parkhurst, whence he never should have come. I shall be miserable if I have the responsibility of his conduct.

The Governor, when he next saw him, agreed to recommend that the Parkhurst authorities take back Robinson.

'I doubt if they will, though,' he said. 'I can't imagine they'll want him back.' He shrugged. 'I don't think we are of much concern to the home authorities. We're on the far side of the world and of little consequence compared to places like India. At best, we won't hear from them for eight months or more. You'll have to care for him until then.'

'I may bring him up to Perth when he's fit. I'm thinking of making a Perth Depot . . . I could use some of those buildings by the mill that were used for the Native Institution. Any lad waiting for reassignment could stay there, and I could keep incorrigibles there until they reform ... set them to some trade. They would be under my constant supervision.'

'Who would supervise them when you are away on your rounds?'

'I thought I could use any good lad waiting for reassignment as a monitor.'

'That might be too much of a risk. Talk to me about it when you've thought it through, and estimated costs. Make sure you won't be taking on too much yourself. You'd have them day and night.'

As Schoales passed through the door, the Governor called him back.

'Mister Schoales, I want you to know that I've admired the way you've conducted yourself under great strain. You have my confidence.'

Schoales felt that part of the burden had lifted.

28

During the next three months, Schoales was glad to be away from Perth most of the time, checking on his lads and dealing with the complaints of some masters about their conduct. Although the autumn and early winter weather had been benign, some journeys were arduous. His nights were often troubled by images of the frail, hooded body of Gavin, turning at the end of the rope, and he woke feeling the chill of the spirit that he had felt on the day of Gavin's execution. On later trips, he carried a flask of whiskey, which gave him some ease.

On return to his office late in June, he was pleased to find a despatch from the Parkhurst authorities to say that they would send no more boys until late in the year. When he had dealt with the accumulated papers, he found a recent map of the colony, and pinned it to the wall. He stuck pins with coloured heads in the map, to show where all the boys were now located.

When he had finished, he picked up a ruler and measured the distances between the northernmost and southernmost pins, and between Fremantle and the easternmost pin. Checking the scale of the map, he calculated that the former was one-hundred miles and the second seventy miles. He then pencilled in the route that he had followed during the past fortnight, zigzagging east-west-east as he had moved north. He then determined that altogether he had ridden four-hundred miles. Some of the route had been through dreary country, with not another house for fifty miles. He returned to his desk to continue writing a memorandum to the Governor:

My absences from Perth are now so frequent & protracted & so uncertain as naturally to interfere with my practice as a Barrister. The very foundation of my practice is the certainty of being found a moments notice, & that foundation, that sole auxiliary source whence I can eke out a subsistence is grievously disturbed ...

He was interrupted by a knock at the door. When he opened it, he found Mrs Symmons on the step, dressed again in riding habit, although she had taken off her jacket.

'I felt lonely,' she said. 'Charles is away again, and I ... we've not seen you for weeks.'

'I've been away most of the time,' Schoales said. 'Since the second shipload of boys came, I've been called away about four times as often. And the distances are much greater.'

He spread his arms, to suggest the distance, and turned to point to the map on the wall. His right arm brushed against Mrs Symmons' breast. She caught her breath and Schoales turned to look at her. She flushed and stared at him intently. He recalled how she always contrived to stand in front of him in the choir, and that she sometimes moved backward and contacted him. He was never sure if the movement was accidental or deliberate. Their voices matched perfectly when they sang duets together – her soprano almost pure, although occasional lower notes had a slightly husky quality, which appealed to him.

Neither of them moved, each knowing that any action was fraught with danger as well as promise.

After a silence that, to both of them, seemed to last for minutes, Schoales spoke huskily, 'Missus Sym ... Joanna ... please don't ever come again on your own. And you must understand that I can't visit you when Charles is away, not even when there are others.'

She backed away, and then turned to hesitate with one hand on the edge of the open door. She looked back at Schoales over her shoulder, who made no move, then pushed the door closed behind her.

Schoales felt abandoned and stood for some time before he began to pace back and forth, until he could force himself to return to writing the memorandum. He detailed the increased distances and travelling times, and the increased costs, which exceeded his travelling allowances. When he had finished, he put down his pen. He suddenly remembered the harrowing image that had haunted some of his nights. When he picked up his pen again, he wrote of the difficulty he had trying to fathom the minds of all the boys in his charge:

... not to say a word on being called on to go through harrowing scenes in a death cell, which is more than probable may be again enacted.

29

During the following week, Schoales prepared a spare room near his office, with a hammock and a small cupboard. He looked forward to having company, even of a troublesome boy, and hoped that it would not be too long before he could fit out the dormitory at the old Native Institution to house other boys. On the following morning, he rode down to the Fremantle Depot to assess whether Robinson was ready to be moved to Perth.

When he arrived there, Mrs Jenkins told him that the boy had absconded again.

'Damn the boy!' he said. 'I wish I could be rid of him. I'll have to get Edar to track him. He might have gone to Pomeroy's place.'

He immediately went to George King's Aboriginal school, as some of the native men might be there hoping for whale meat. He engaged Edar and another native, and said that he would go part of the way with them, until they were certain where the boy was heading.

The two natives took some time to find Robinson's footprints on a patch of soft sand about a hundred yards from the Depot. Fortunately, it was not a windy day, so the footprints had not been blown away. It took them half an hour to find that he had zigzagged through the streets of the town to the eastern outskirts. They frequently lost the trail where the boy had crossed hard ground or paving.

At one point, Edar stopped and said, 'Boy running. He fall.' He pointed to scuff marks in the sand. As he moved on, he said, 'Boy limping.' The prints of Robinson's left foot were less distinct than those of his right foot.

The trail became relatively easy to follow on sandy ground. Robinson was following the track along the south of the river leading inland.

'As I thought,' Schoales said, 'he's heading toward Pomeroy's. He's forgotten that the Pomeroys have gone to York. You go ahead, Edar, as quickly as you can. I'll wait for you at the Depot.' He hoped that Robinson would not panic when he found that there was no one at Pomeroy's place.

Edar and his companion walked away quickly and broke into a trot whenever the trail was clear.

Late in the afternoon, the two natives returned to the Depot with the boy. They had found him lying in front of the cottage at Pomeroy's farm. Schoales handed each of them a shilling and, grasping Robinson by one shoulder, marched him inside.

'What am I to do with you, Ned? I've lost patience with you,' he said. 'I keep trying to help you, but you've let me down again.'

Robinson scowled. 'I won't go to anyone I don't like.'

'I haven't forced you to go to anyone that you didn't like. Mister Austin was kind to you, I thought.'

'He caned me.'

'Only when you ran away, so he had just cause.'

'I wanted to see Mister Pomeroy.'

'Have you forgotten that I told you he went to York? I don't like doing this, but you must be taught to behave.'

Schoales took down the cane from the top of the cupboard. When he turned back, he saw that the boy had a pocket-knife in his hand, with the blade open. As Schoales approached him, he slashed twice at this throat, to the left and to the right, and then dropped to the floor. Schoales flung away the cane and called out, 'Missus Jenkins, bring some bandages quickly.'

The two cuts, about three inches long, were superficial but bleeding. Schoales bandaged the boy's throat as tightly as he dare, not wishing to interfere with the boy's breathing.

'I'll take him to Doctor Ferguson,' he said.

He picked up the small boy and carried him from the Depot to Dr Ferguson's surgery. Fortunately, the doctor was there.

Ferguson removed the bandages and examined the wounds. 'Well, they're not deep enough to need stitches. The knife must've been blunt, thank goodness.'

'Either that, or it was just a desperate gesture.'

'I'll keep him here until the wounds heal,' Ferguson said.

'I'm tired of being responsible for him. I've told the authorities back home that I think he's mentally unfit and should be taken back there, or committed to care.'

'On the evidence of this act, I agree with you. I'll make a report in those terms,' Ferguson said.

'I hope that someone'll listen this time,' Schoales said.

Schoales spent the night at the Crown and Thistle, as night would fall before he could reach Perth, and he did not feel ready to make the journey alone while he was depressed by the day's events. The glass of sherry that he had before the meal, and the half bottle of wine that he drank with it, helped him to sleep.

Afterword

Schoales was tormented frequently by Robinson's continued lapses, and was never able to have him returned to Parkhurst. The tone of his frequent written requests to the Governor demonstrated increasing desperation to be rid of the boy. Another batch of boys arrived in December 1844, so that he had sixty boys in his charge. He also had to admit to the failure of the Central Depot in Perth. He was away too frequently to supervise the boys housed there. Moreover, when he was in residence, he was called away frequently at night because one or more of the boys had committed crimes at houses in the town. He tried again to get approval for his proposal for a farm, where incorrigible lads could be under constant supervision, but the home authorities did not respond.

In 1846, Schoales's health was deteriorating, although by May, his friend Lefroy reported in his diary that he was better. This may have been the early signs of alcoholism.

In October of that year, one of his wards was tried for the rape of the eight-year-old daughter of his employer. At that time, rape was still a capital offence, and Schoales faced the prospect of another of his charges being hanged. However, the boy pleaded guilty and was sentenced to imprisonment.

Hutt's term as Governor ended in February of that year. In November, Peter Broun, who had been Colonial Secretary since 1829, died. The governance of the colony was being transformed, at a time when Schoales's physical and mental states were deteriorating.

Hutt was succeeded by Colonel Andrew Clarke, who committed Robinson to the permanent care of the Colonial Surgeon Superintendent as a mental patient.

However, Clarke responded to increasing complaints of some of the boys about Schoales's handling of their moneys, by setting up a formal inquiry.

Schoales was only thirty-seven when he died on 10 April, before the committee of inquiry could submit its report.

The committee found Schoales's accounts in disarray. There were discrepancies from a few shillings to a few pounds in the accounts of forty-nine of the seventy-four boys then in his care, and Schoales faced the possibility of being found guilty of embezzlement. Although the committee, reporting after his death, did not determine whether the deficiencies were due to negligence or embezzlement, they did order sequestration of Schoales's estate so that the boys could be compensated.

Lefroy did not hear of his friend's death until a fortnight after it occurred. He wrote in his journal:

Heard that poor Schoales was dead, another victim of drink brought on by disappointment of this place. Building castles in the air, so spending the money of young men he had in his charge. Things not turning out as he fully expected, he was not able to pay them & they, no one or two of them, accused him with swindling. It played on his mind until he turned to drink, the last resource of young men in this place. No death since I came here I felt but his ... Poor Mrs

Nash, I pity her from my heart. They were so fond of one another. Oh that day of trial and separation from those we perhaps too dearly love awaits us all & may God prepare us for it. One of the few gentlemen &, though the lying slander of the world has passed not over him, I believe him to have been strictly honourable but of no business.

Acknowledgements

My interest in John Gavin's story was first roused by reading
Paul Buddee's *The Fate of the Artful Dodger* (1984, St George
Books, Perth, Western Australia), which led me to research in
the Western Australian State Records Office. More recently,
I benefited from the generosity of Andrew Gill, who shared
his knowledge gleaned from research for his magisterial
study, *Forced Labour for the West: Parkhurst Convicts 'apprenticed'
in Western Australia 1842–1851*, (1997, Blatellae Books,
Maylands, Western Australia). Gill corrects some errors in
Buddee's work, and he may disagree with some of my inter-
pretations of events.

My thanks also to Ryan Paine for his patient and meti-
culous editing of this work.

Poinciana
Jane Turner Goldsmith

ISBN 978 1 86254 699 8

Catherine Piron is in Noumea, searching for traces of the father she barely remembers. She meets journalist Henri Boulez, her only lead in a foreign country. Their journey into the remote regions of New Caledonia uncovers an extraordinary story that, like the island itself, brille à la fois claire et noire au soleil – shimmers light and dark in the sun.

For more information visit www.wakefieldpress.com.au

One Common Enemy

The Laconia incident: A survivor's memoir
Jim McLoughlin with David Gibb

ISBN 978 1 86254 690 5

'I'll see the world,' Jim McLoughlin told his parents as he set off to join the Royal Navy in 1939. 'It'll be fun.'

Months later, this Liverpool lad was sailing to war aboard the massive battleship HMS *Valiant*. He saw some of the world, but it wasn't fun.

In *One Common Enemy*, he recounts how the chaos and carnage of war at sea in the Norwegian and Mediterranean campaigns led him to a fateful rendezvous with a much-loved ship from his boyhood, the passenger liner *Laconia*. Nostalgia turned to disaster when *Laconia* was torpedoed by a German U-boat in the South Atlantic. Despite a remarkable rescue attempt by a courageous, compassionate foe, Jim was condemned to a drifting lifeboat and a harrowing voyage of death and madness.

One Common Enemy is a story of a desperate personal battle for survival, but also a moving narrative of innocence lost and a lifelong battle with confronting memories.

For more information visit www.wakefieldpress.com.au

Calum's Road
Roger Hutchinson

ISBN 978 1 86254 739 1

At the age of 56, Calum MacLeod, the last man left in northern Raasay, an island in a tiny archipelago situated off the Isle of Skye, set about single-handedly constructing the road others deemed 'impossible'. It would become a romantic, quixotic venture, a kind of sculpture; an obsessive work of art so perfect in every gradient, culvert and supporting wall that its creation occupied almost twenty years of his life. In *Calum's Road*, award-winning author and journalist Roger Hutchinson, recounts the extraordinary story of this remarkable man's devotion to his visionary project.

'Wonderful, elegant and serious.' – *Telegraph*

'A story of heroic anti-authoritarian, anti-socialist, anti-mainland, anti-council, anti-bureaucratic bloody-mindedness.' – *Spectator*

'Perceptive and beautifully written.' – *Country Life*

For more information visit www.wakefieldpress.com.au

Wakefield Press is an independent publishing and
distribution company based in Adelaide, South Australia.
We love good stories and publish beautiful books.
To see our full range of titles, please visit our website at
www.wakefieldpress.com.au.